"When I say *recon*, I mean it in the purest sense," Track said

"By the book? No combat no matter what?"

"Exactly," Track said. "I want to avoid any open contact until we get our bearings. We'll have to find a good observation point, then watch what's going on."

"Cover is sparse in that area," Steve warned him.

Track shrugged. "Well, pal, you never promised this thing would be easy."

"Yeah," Steve said, "I hate like hell to sound ominous, but there's an old Apache war saying that's been running through my head since last night."

"What's that?" Track asked.

The Indian smiled. *"It's a good day to die,"* he said.

Introducing Patrick Andrews

"I've been writing in the western and action-adventure markets for years, and one goal I'd set for myself was to join my good friend Gar Wilson on the Gold Eagle team," says Patrick Andrews.

Pat attended the 1985 Mack Bolan Convention in San Francisco, where he met many of Gold Eagle's most loyal fans and was able to get valuable insight into what readers wanted to see in the Track series.

An ex-paratrooper, and holder of the army's highest jump rating, the master parachutist badge, Pat has served with some of the United States Army's most elite units from the 187th Airborne Regimental Combat Team and the 82nd Airborne Division in the Regulars, to earning his green beret as a member of the 12th Special Forces Group (Airborne) of the Reserves. He retired from soldiering after twenty-three years of service.

Pat Andrews is the author of numerous paperback books and writes articles on military history for *Soldier of Fortune* and *Infantry.* He likes to spend his Saturday afternoons at the shooting range with Gar Wilson.

TRACK
The Ghost Dancers

PATRICK ANDREWS

A GOLD EAGLE BOOK FROM
WORLDWIDE
TORONTO • NEW YORK • LONDON • PARIS
AMSTERDAM • STOCKHOLM • HAMBURG
ATHENS • MILAN • TOKYO • SYDNEY

First edition February 1986

ISBN 0-373-62011-X

Printed in Canada.

PROLOGUE

Cumulus clouds floated with an eerie laziness through the highest altitudes of the desert's night sky. Although the vapory formations were strung out and thinly spaced, now and then they would momentarily blot out the moon's bright light.

The Apache warrior, despite the night's pinching cold, squatted as motionless as a lizard. He was concealed within the shadows flowing outward from a tall stand of boulders. His dress was traditional—a loose calico shirt, leather vest, loincloth and knee-high moccasins. A canvas bandolier holding a couple of dozen lethal cartridges hung across one shoulder. The rifle he held added to his ominous appearance as did the patterns of war paint he had streaked across his copper-colored face.

The warrior remained in the position for another hour. His passive face showed only a flicker of interest when finally the sound of a horse's hoof striking a stone cracked through the dark silence. The Apache knew from which direction the animal and its rider were approaching; in fact, he had been waiting for them. When he could see the shadowy figure, he brought the rifle up in a single motion, the sights instantly aligned.

Another few seconds passed as the muzzle of the weapon continued to point unwaveringly toward the human target. When the right moment arrived, the trigger finger tightened quickly, smoothly. Hammer hit firing pin, firing pin hit primer, and the resulting explosion drove the .30-.30 bullet down the rifle barrel to spiral across the short space and slam into the victim's left cheek.

The slug, a soft-nosed hunting round, blossomed wide and careered slightly upward before exploding out of the man's right ear leaving a hole big enough to poke a medium-sized water gourd into.

The warrior stood up and watched dully as the frightened horse galloped off into the southern-Arizona night. Then he walked to the cadaver. His moccasined feet made no sound as he trod lightly across the hard-packed, sandy soil.

Using the carbine barrel, he rolled his victim over. The Indian looked down and could see the man's features, now caved in around the shattered facial bone along the left side. The Apache felt a surge of personal pride above and beyond the fact he had just killed a man he hated. At that particular time, he was more pleased by the means than the end. He had figured out the proper angle and line of flight of the bullet's path through sheer instinct. Not too very long ago he would have solved this problem of distance/trajectory through the skillful application of computer programming and advanced calculus in his now-abandoned profession as an aerospace engineer.

He laughed aloud.

The warrior was glad the skills of his forefathers still danced through his soul.

1

The DC-10 swung into the proper approach to the San Diego International Airport. There was plenty of room in the flight corridor to allow the pilot to stay out of Mexican air space and also avoid the traffic patterns of Brown Field near San Ysidro.

The senior flight attendant, surprisingly large breasted for such a svelt woman, had just finished her pre-landing speech to the passengers. As she replaced the microphone, she took a quick but interested look at one of the male passengers. She and the other attendants had instantly noticed his attractiveness when he boarded. Taking advantage of her rank, she had quickly rearranged the serving roster so that she was able to wait on him for lunch as well as drinks before and after the meal.

The passenger, a well-muscled man with brown hair and blue eyes, stretched out his six-foot length as much as he was able. He caught the woman looking at him, and he smiled. Her gaze didn't falter, its boldness making Dan Track look forward even more to their date that night.

The attendant walked slowly down the aisle, checking each seat belt. She stopped at Dan's seat and leaned over as if to help him adjust the buckle. "See you at eight, right?"

"Sure, Madeline," Track said. "Unless you want me to wait for you at the airport."

"I can't get away for a couple of hours," Madeline said pouting a little. "I have to turn in a damned logistics report on the food and drinks consumed during the flight." She reached in his jacket pocket and pulled out the slip of paper that bore her address and phone number. "I just wanted to make sure you hadn't lost it."

"Are you kidding?" he asked. "I'd sooner lose my luggage."

"Flatterer!" she whispered, then moved on.

The man beside Track listened to the exchange with a sad smile, wishing he were twenty years younger and as many pounds lighter. He rubbed a pudgy hand across the baldness of his head. Then he sighed and said, "You don't waste time, do you, buddy?"

Dan Track smiled at him. "This old world turns fast," he said. "I can't let a second go by without some sort of effort."

Track was indeed a fast worker. This was as much from habit as from eagerness to have some long intimate moments with the eager flight attendant. His line of work rarely granted him the luxury of being able to carefully and leisurely pursue the women he found attractive. Courtships for Dan Track were hurried activities carried on with a minimum of wasted time and a maximum of accomplishments. Thus, he had rushed her, blitzed her with charm, leaving the young woman surprised and breathless. The tactic rarely failed.

Track wasn't working on this particular trip. He had been contacted by an old army buddy by telephone only two days previously. The ex-comrade-in-arms, named Steve Aguila, had invited him out to San Diego. Pleased and surprised to hear from a good friend he hadn't seen in several years, Track had been glad he'd had the time to spare. Camaraderie and friendship, formed under dangerous, adverse conditions, lasts a lifetime. He and Steve had grown close in Saigon during a campaign against a powerful and vicious gang of dope smugglers and white slavers, who had ruled in the Cholon district of that city for almost a dozen years.

Track, a member of the army's Criminal Investigation Division, had met Steve in what turned out to be a happy coincidence generated by military bureaucracy. Steve, a Green Beret temporarily assigned to the CID as an asset, had an aggressive temperament and coolness under stress that matched Track's. The two became a team, going after the Oriental hoods until the last one went down screaming his defiant hatred and fear in a stinking Saigon back street.

The fact that Steve had been an absolutely ferocious fighter hadn't surprised Track. After all, his friend was a full-blooded Apache Indian.

Dan watched Madeline walk past him again to return to her seat. Then he let his gaze drift out the window. He watched as the aircraft eased down and the view shifted from Balboa Park, to San Diego's Old Town and finally to the buildings of General Dynamic's Convair Division before the tires squeeled onto the concrete of the runway.

The usual disorganized milling around followed as the passengers struggled out of their seats. They pulled personal luggage from the overhead racks before beginning the slow walk to the door and ramp that would lead them into the bowels of the airport.

Track kept to his seat, having only to turn sideways to let his overweight seatmate struggle over his feet, then waited as the crowd jostled its way good-naturedly off the aircraft. When there was plenty of room for a leisurely stroll toward the exit, Track got his small valise and walked up to the stowage compartment where he'd hung his garment bag.

He paused at the door and quickly pecked Madeline on the cheek. She responded with an instinctive kiss on the lips. It, too, was hasty, but the rapid dart of her tongue left a lingering promise.

"I'll see you later," Track said.

He walked down the debarking ramp and out into the corridor where a sign directed him toward the street. His walk, seemingly leisurely, was silently efficient, each stride carrying him at a ground-eating gait. As he approached the revolving door that would admit him into the waiting area, he caught sight of the grinning, dark countenance of Steve Aguila.

Memories of the deafening reports of firearms, the smell of burned cordite and the muffled groans of wounded and dying men bleeding on the dank concrete and mud alleys of Saigon flooded through Track's mind.

Steve was a compact, muscular, five feet nine inches, with slightly bowed legs. When his features were lit up with a wide grin he seemed friendly and pleasant. But in times of bad temper, Steve's face was an immobile mask of silent fury. Even when in deep thought, he could appear frightening to the faint of heart.

The Apache took the valise in his left hand and held out his right for Track to shake. "How're you doing, sir?"

Track, an ex-major, laughed aloud. "Jesus! You never called me that when we were in the army. What's got you started now?"

"I figured I owed you at least one," Steve said. "But no salutes, huh?"

"Right," Track agreed. "I remember you did give me one—the last time we saw each other."

"It was one of the few I meant," Steve said. "C'mon. I've got us a couple of rooms at the Sheraton Airport Hotel."

"Hotel?" Track asked. He paused, puzzled. "Now where'd I get the idea you lived here?"

Steve shrugged. "Hell, I don't know. I just wanted to meet you here."

"Any particular reason?"

"San Diego is a nice place," Steve said. But he added more seriously, "I'll explain later. But, just to set the record straight, I live in Arizona."

"What're we going to do here?" asked Track. "Have a deep-sea fishing vacation?"

"We're not staying in San Diego," Steve said. "We're going to Arizona."

Track shook his head. "What the hell did you have me fly all the way over here for? We could've met in Phoenix, Tucson, or—"

"I have a good reason for getting together here," Steve said. There was an edge of seriousness in his voice. Then he turned and hurried out toward the taxi stand.

Track felt a surge of the old excitement, rather close to déjà-vu, with the taste of danger added. It was exactly like the empty feeling in his gut when they would leave the headquarters building at Peterson Field to head for an operation in the Cholon.

And Track knew he wouldn't be seeing Madeline that night—or ever, probably.

2

The leggy cocktail waitress reminded Track so much of Madeline that he felt a stirring deep in his male soul, but he fought down his natural desires and ordered a Scotch and soda with a bold look at the cleavage her scant costume proffered. Steve, on the other hand, settled for a light beer with only a casual glance at her. Track couldn't help but note his friend's distracted manner.

He looked across the booth at his old buddy. Despite Steve's muscularity, he was trim and obviously in shape. "Drinking light brew? You don't look like you need to cut back calories, Slim."

Steve smiled. "The white man's firewater is no good for this Injun. I'm not ready to bloat up quite yet."

The waitress returned with their drinks. "If you need anything else, just wave," she said in a low voice, throwing Track a smile.

"Right," Track said agreeably.

"Don't be bashful," she said. The woman paused long enough to make sure Track caught her smile, then sauntered off to another table.

"I see you still got the touch," Steve remarked.

"I hope to hang on to it to the bitter end, too," Track said. He took another look at the woman. "Man! She's got legs all the way up—"

"To her ass," Steve intoned. He took a quick sip of his beer.

Track eyed him carefully. "I get the feeling you're impatient about something, old buddy."

"Hey, no shit?"

Track could feel that his friend had been reining in hard on something since his arrival at the airport. "You're up to your eyeballs in alligators, Steve. Need somebody to drain the swamp?"

"I need help," Steve said plaintively. "I'm going to ask a favor of you—a humungus one."

"You call—I haul," Track said. "Fill me in."

Steve lifted a hand in a restraining gesture. "Don't commit yourself till I've given you the big picture."

Track took a swallow of the drink. "I'm waiting."

Steve hesitated. "I'm not sure how to begin this particular briefing—but I suppose the best way is to let you know that I'm chief of police on the Llanero Apache Reservation."

Track nodded. "I'm impressed. And I presume this problem has something to do with your work." He tried to lighten both the conversation and the mood. "Who do you want me to help you arrest—Geronimo or Cochise?"

"Geronimo," Steve answered.

"Geronimo who?"

"Actually, his name is Geronimo Ferril," Steve started to explain. "But sometimes I'd swear the son of a bitch is the original Geronimo reincarnated."

"Whoa, pal! You're running this one past me too fast."

"Let me get this out in my own way, okay?" Steve asked.

Track leaned back in the booth. "Have at it. I won't say a thing till you're finished."

Steve took another sip of beer, then began with a brief history of his people.

THE LLANERO APACHES were distant—and unfriendly—cousins of their brethren, the Chiricahua and Mescalero Apaches. Blood feuds, stretching back eons, had kept the smaller tribe of Llaneros in constant battle with the others, though not as much as with the Mexicans. They were, however, always friendly with another tribe of Apaches known as the Bedonkohe.

The Bedonkohe had their own antagonists. They hated the Mexicans in the state of Sonora, but traded with those in Chihuahua. For the Llaneros, the opposite was true. They traveled throughout Sonora unmolested, but any forays into Chihuahua meant instant trouble—although the fact they only went there to raid might have had something to do with the unfriendly welcome accorded them by the inhabitants.

These topsy-turvy relationships were the reason for an unusual trading deal between the Llaneros and Bedonkohes. If the Bedonkohes had something they could get good prices for in Sonora, their friends the Llaneros made the deal for them. The Bedonkohes did the same with Llanero goods in Chihuahua.

It was one of those peaceful commercial missions that proved to be the springboard for launching Apaches, Mexicans and Americans into one of the bloodiest Indian wars in the history of western North America.

During the trapping season of 1857-58, the Llaneros had enjoyed good luck in the mountains of Arizona. The best prices for their pelts could be had in Chihuahua, but they were unable to go there because of the unfriendly situation. As was customary, they asked a group of Bedonkohes if they would be kind enough to take the goods in and make the deal for them. The Bedonkohes agreed. Among those making the trip was a young man named Geronimo.

The Apaches preferred to take their families with them when it was possible, and the women and kids liked the opportunity for a change of scenery too. So a group of them traveled to the town of Janos in Sonora to do the trading for the Llaneros.

After leaving a small guard with the women and children in the makeshift camp, the men went into town to trade the furs and enjoy a few drinks. When both business and diversions were satisfactorily completed, the Apaches left Janos. They were on their way back to camp when they met a small group of their women and children fleeing from the impromptu bivouac. These noncombatants told a horrible story of a sneak attack and massacre by a troop of Mexican Irregulars. The Apache warriors hurried back to find out what had happened to their families.

The encampment was strewn with the mutilated corpses of their relatives. The Mexican guerrillas, from another area, had sneaked in from the west in the glare of the setting sun. After killing the men guarding the camp, they attacked the noncombatants, striking down children with the same gusto as adults. After the furor died down, the Mexicans scalped the dead, taking the bloody trophies for the bounty offered by the Coahuilan governor over in the next state.

Among the grief-stricken men was Geronimo. He had lost his wife and three children. The sadness that tore at his heart eventually evolved into rage. The history books carry the grisly results of the frenzied lust for revenge that spilled over from the Mexicans to the white settlers in the southwest.

When the news of the atrocity got back to the Llaneros, they felt a great deal of responsibility for what had happened. After all, their friends were doing them a favor when the tragedy occurred. The Llaneros showed the depth of their feelings of remorse by spending the next twenty-eight years supporting Geronimo's war against his enemies.

Although the whole tribe never participated in the warfare as a group, there were always Llanero warriors along on Bedonkohes' raids. They even patched up the hard feelings they had for the Chiricahuas and Mescaleros, developing new shared hatreds for the White Mountain Apaches who served as scouts for the U.S. Army.

In 1886, when Geronimo surrendered to General Nelson A. Miles, the Apaches were shipped off to Florida while the proud Geronimo went to Fort Sill in Oklahoma Territory to finish out his life.

The Llaneros, since there was no evidence or record of the entire tribe's making war against the whites at any one time, were treated slightly better. They were put on a miserable reservation to be turned into farmers and shepherds.

And there they stayed, right up to contemporary times.

TRACK FINISHED his second drink. "An interesting story, I agree," he said. "But what the hell has that got to do with us meeting here in San Diego?"

"You know what a ghost dance is?" Steve asked.

"Some Indian religious ceremony," Track answered.

"Yeah," Steve said. "The Sioux and other Plains Indians are best known for them, but we Apaches had a few too. They were big medicine for resurrecting Indian dead."

Track began to recall some of his American history. "Yeah. It's coming back to me now. The idea was that all these Indians suddenly coming to life would be enough to outnumber the whites and drive them out of their land."

"Yep," Steve said. "And right now I've got one hell of a ghost dance on my hands."

Track shrugged. "What's the harm in that?"

"Plenty," Steve said. He leaned forward. "This guy Geronimo Ferril showed up on the reservation about four or five months ago. A mean-looking dude—"

"Apache?"

"All the way—and a Llanero to boot," Steve responded. "He's been back before. He's a Ph.D., and he'd been working on our people's history and folklore for several years. This time he didn't do much at first. Then he started acting real odd. He built a wickiup and wore the clothes of the old people—y'know, breechcloths, moccasins and all that. Most of the folks figured he'd turned eccentric, or maybe was trying to be trendy about his ethnicity. Then he started to talk to the old people. Naturally, this guy really had his Apache legends down cold. The oldsters in their eighties and nineties could barely remember some of those stories, but this guy knew 'em all—and could repeat each one word for word every time without varying a goddamn syllable."

"The guy has a hell of a memory."

"Yeah," Steve said with a mirthless laugh, "and he did it in fluent Apache. There's not a whole lot of people around—including me—that speak the language too well anymore."

"I'm impressed," Track said. He noted Steve's empty glass. "Ready for a refill?"

"Yeah."

Track signaled the waitress. She glided over in a hip-swinging stride that gave him a sweet ache. Track smiled. "Two more of the same."

"Sure, and remember what I said," she remarked going back to the bar, "don't be bashful."

Steve grinned shaking his head. "I'd worry about you, but I've never known even the notorious Dan Track to put pussy ahead of a job."

"What's the problem?" Dan asked. "We're spending the night here anyway."

"Nope," Steve said. "I'll need your answer tonight. I hate to rush you, but I don't have a hell of a lot of time."

"Damn!" Track said.

"One way or another, I'm driving over across the state line tonight."

"Are you kidding?" Track asked. "First you have us meet way over here in San Diego when you live in Arizona, then we check into a hotel—where, evidently, you aren't planning to stay. What gives, Steve?"

"I'm getting to that," Steve said. "I'm covering my tracks like the devil himself was after me. And maybe he is."

The waitress returned with their drinks. Track took a second to play another hand in his silent game with her, then reluctantly took his eyes off the woman. "Okay, Steve. Charge ahead."

"This guy got to the point where whole crowds of people would gather in front of that fucking wickiup of his every night to listen to his goddamned lectures. He even eventually took a young girl for a wife."

"Sounds like he was really settling in," Track said. "So far he doesn't seem too sinister to me."

"At that point he wasn't," Steve admitted. "But then he started attracting attention from some of the younger guys. Being an Apache is a big deal to us, Dan. It's more than a tribal name. It stands for our religion, our beliefs, philosophies—hell, our souls! So when Ferril started telling tales of the ancient warriors and their deeds, the young dudes ate it up. Some of them started using the ancient names. I wasn't alarmed about it. I thought it was just great. I'm sure as hell proud to be an Apache. And fighting is in our hearts. All the guys that go into the service sign on as marines or paratroopers or rangers—all that gung-ho stuff. We take to it like ducks to water."

"You sure as hell do," Track said, from experience.

"Then Ferril picked a few of the guys who were really going for his gab, and he took them on a retreat up to our sacred areas. In the last few years only some of the old men ever went up there. Anyhow, Ferril and the others fasted and prayed to the gods. In other words, they made medicine, and when they came back down you would've sworn they'd stepped out of the pages of time. Track, I'm telling you they were Apaches—*Apaches*, man!"

Track looked directly into Steve's deep, black eyes. They seemed to snap and sparkle in intensity. "Go on," he said.

"The other young guys crowded around them, and Geronimo made a speech. He really got into the ghost dance bit. He couldn't promise to bring back the dead or anything like that, but he said the ceremony would recharge the Llaneros' spirits—really turn them back into Apaches."

"Again, pardon me, but I don't see much harm in all this," Track said.

"The next thing on his agenda was that we declare ourselves to be an independent nation and get the U.S. Government the hell off our backs."

"Well, given the way things are on the reservations, I can't say I'm surprised."

"Look, I'm pissed off about the way we Indians are treated too," Steve said. "We're hemmed in by treaties and surrender terms that were made a hundred years ago. But I'm going to fight back within the system. Hell, I'm studying law at night at the University of Arizona in Tucson. I figure I'll be able to take some of those old deals between us and the Great White Father in Washington and rip 'em to shreds in the courts."

"That's a hell of an admirable goal!" Track said. "Your way sounds better than Ferril's. Couldn't you win the young guys over?"

"Hell, no! Ferril's group even grew in numbers," Steve said. "And to top it off, some of the guys who had gone off to school and lived far away in cities working as professionals heard about this stuff. A lot of them came back to see what was going on. Most stayed. I wasn't concerned until Ferril and his guys started picking on the people that didn't believe in them."

"That's bad," Track said.

"It got worse. They went beyond ass-kicking and zapped a couple of their more vocal opponents." Steven paused, his voice lowering under the weight of the hatred in it. "Then they got a couple of my policemen—I couldn't stand for that."

"Okay," Track said. "That's serious. So you call in the cops—Feds or State or whoever can do the job—and you round up these crazies and that's the end of it."

Steve shook his head. "No fucking way. I'm an Apache. I don't want a bunch of outsiders sticking their noses into our affairs."

"Okay," Track said, "So, you're the chief of police, use the rest of your own men."

"They're all dead now," Steve said coldly, "all six of them. They got the last guy a few nights ago. I had to evade-and-escape my own ass out of there."

"Damn!"

"I'm all alone—until now."

"And you called me."

Steve smiled. "What's that song Sonny and Cher sang? 'I Got You, Babe'? Well, I used my police contacts and went through the CIA. They knew where you were, and I figured you'd been keeping real active in those things you love the best."

Track fully realized the seriousness of Steve's position, and knew the Apache was committed to fighting this Ferril no matter what. "I presume, naturally, that you want me to throw in with you."

Steve hesitated. "Now that I'm eyeball to eyeball with you, I know I shouldn't have asked."

Track looked directly into his friend's eyes. "You damned well better have asked!"

"I can't pay you any money, Dan," Steve said. "There's no kind of profit in this at all. And the chances of pulling it off are the same as the proverbial snowball in hell."

"You say you don't want any outsiders," Track said. "Where do I fit in?"

"You're the only man in the world I'd ask to lend me a hand," Steve said. "But, honest to God, I won't hold it against you if you say no."

"Maybe *you* won't, but *I* sure as hell will," Track said. "I'm in."

Steve smiled gratefully. "You crazy bastard!"

"Just how many are we facing?" Track asked.

"About a hundred fighters with their women and children."

"Two against a hundred?" Track's serious expression dissolved into a vicious grin. "Sounds like a hell of a good time."

"We've always had fun together," Steve said with a laugh.

Track finished his drink and banged the glass on the table. "C'mon! Let's get a bottle and go up to our room. We've got some serious boozing and talking to do."

"There'll be a hell of a lot more talking than boozing when I finish filling you in," Steve said.

As the two friends walked out the door of the bar, the waitress turned from her station where the bartender was mixing an order for her. "Why are the good-looking ones always running out on me?"

"I've seen hard-asses like them before, baby. When I was in the army I worked in NCO clubs over in Nam," the man said swishing the stirrer in the drink. "I'd watch them Green Berets and Long Range Patrol guys come in from the boonies. You could see what kind of stone-hard dudes they were by looking at their eyes. They had cold expressions that didn't say nothing, but man, wherever they went it was bad news for somebody."

The woman looked toward the door. "I wonder what they're up to."

"Consider yourself lucky it don't concern you. They're trouble for anybody in their lives—and that goes double for each other!"

3

Firelight danced across the dark, hollowed features of the three men. Two watched in wakeful interest, despite their fatigue, as their companion slowly stirred the *sopa* cooking over the coals of the campfire.

The cook ran his tongue along his dry lips. *"Va estar lista en uno minutos mas,"* he said, announcing that their meal would be ready within a few minutes.

The three were bone-weary, having spent several nights traveling across the Great Sonoran Desert. Night spared them the awful heat of the day, but the darkness offered more than comforting coolness—it gave them cover from the ever vigilant U.S. Border Patrol. The three were illegals, making a physically demanding journey that would carry them deep into the rich land of the *gringos*. That was where the jobs were; a place where a man could do the work the *norteamericanos* would not lower themselves to do. The Mexicans did it at coolie wages, enough to buy *tortillas* and beans to feed a faraway but well-loved family.

These three were penniless farmers from Sinaloa. Their home village was so poor that cash was a rare thing to be had there. The economy was based more on barter than money, and they could not afford to pay the outrageous demands of the "coyotes"—the professional smugglers of human beings who took money to bring aliens without papers into America.

The youngest of the trio, a wiry teenager named Javier, stared at the cooking food. *"Como tengo hambre,"* he remarked.

The oldest of their small fraternity, a middle-aged man named Guillermo, gently scolded him and the other. "Speak English, even if it not so good, eh?"

Javier grinned sheepishly. "I am sorry." He cleared his throat and spoke again, repeating himself in a language foreign to him. "How hungry I am."

Mario, the third farmer, only a few years older than Javier, pulled a crumpled pack of Pegasus cigarettes from the pocket of his faded denim jacket. "What differ'nce it make?" He stuck a manzanita twig into the fire and lit it. The tobacco of the cheap cigarette flamed up when he applied the fire to it. "We work with other *mexicanos* anyhow."

"Yes," agreed Guillermo, "but if we need directions and have to ask an *americano* and we do it in English pretty good, he maybe won't think we are *sin papeles*—I mean, without papers."

"¡Mierda!" swore Mario as a way of arguing. It was a shame that as a good Catholic he was to die with an obscenity on his lips.

The bullet hit him dead center in the forehead, flopping him over on his back. His legs flew straight up, then he fell back into an undignified posture.

Guillermo instinctively leaped to his feet. The movement was so quick and unexpected that one bullet passed harmlessly in front of his belly. The second hit his elbow and spun him around to catch a third in the shoulder. It careened off the clavicle and plowed downward through his lungs and into his intestines. He sat down, hemorrhaging internally while blood gushed from his mouth and nose.

Javier, the most agile, managed to run a full five yards before three of the five bullets fired at him struck him, almost simultaneously, in the middle of the back. His spine snapped, and he died instantly without pain.

Guillermo, on the other hand, wasn't to be quite so lucky. A strong man, despite his small size, he managed to get to his feet. Going deep into shock, he watched dully as the Apaches stepped from the darkness into the weak light afforded by the campfire. The *campesino* sensed his impending doom, and he spoke out weakly yet with machismo, saying, "I will show you how a brave Mexican dies."

Guillermo was so dazed he wasn't even able to focus on the rifle butt that was swung at his head. He crashed to the ground and thrashed helplessly until the effects of his shattered skull finally killed him.

A half dozen painted Apache warriors stared down at the three dead men. A slight rustle announced the arrival of another warrior. They respectfully stepped aside to allow him to stand in their midst. The new arrival was short and extremely muscular. His skin was a deep brown, and his eyes were locked in a permanent frown. The mouth was no more than a slash under his hawkbill nose.

He pointed at the dead men. "You did well," said Geronimo Ferril. "Remember to hate the Mexicans even more than the whites. They've mistreated our people much longer."

The warriors raised their rifles above their heads and shouted an enthusiastic response.

"But hate Apache traitors even more," Ferril said. "They are like pumas who devour their own young. Perverted and untrustworthy, they have to be destroyed before all others."

"Yeh-ta-hey!" the warriors bellowed.

"We will draw strength and cunning from the ghost dance ceremony. The medicine will establish a bond with the spirits of our ancestors. When they look down upon us, our generation will be honored by the blood of our enemies we have spilled."

Again the Apaches shouted out, *"Yeh-ta-hey!"*

The cry echoed out of the mountains and across the desert below like the scream of a diving eagle.

A BLOOD-RED SUN eased above the horizon to shine onto Dan Track's face.

He and Steve Aguila had left the hotel a few hours earlier. After leaving the bar, they had gone to the room Steve had rented for them. Following a period of intense talk, the two had decided not to waste any more time. Track, who had not unpacked his own bags, waited while Steve threw the few things he'd brought into a small suitcase. Then, checking out quickly with a curious desk clerk, they went to the parking lot for Steve's rented car.

Driving east on Interstate 8, they left San Diego and climbed into the mountains that sealed in the scorching winds of the desert on the east—sparing San Diego the blazing hell of desert heat in the summer—while blocking out the cooling sea breezes from the west.

Winding down into the Imperial Valley, the two friends talked only intermittently as they let their minds settle into the trip. The rented Honda Accord made lulling sounds as its rubber hummed against the long slab of concrete that snaked straight out across the desert like a serpent from another world.

Steve, who had never been very fond of driving, gladly traded off with Track when they reached El Centro. Now, ten miles on the other side of Yuma, Track took the wheel, enjoying the feel of commanding the machine even though it wasn't a high-powered car. He was also able to ignore the fifty-five mph speed limit. If an Arizona State Policeman stopped them, all Steve had to do was flash his chief's badge, and they would be able to speed off on their "official business."

It was midmorning when they reached Eloy where they changed over to Interstate 10. "How about some breakfast?" Steve asked.

"Call it brunch," Track said checking his watch.

"Call it anything you want," Steve said. "It's chow time." He whistled out "Mess Call," a tune welcome to the ears of countless generations of soldiers.

Track drove through the town and finally pulled into a small roadside diner on the other side. "How's this place look?"

"Great," Steve said. He pulled on the door handle and stepped out. The blast of desert heat almost made him gasp. "Damn!" he swore. "Air conditioning can make a wimp out of you in a real short span of time, can't it?"

Track, standing on the other side of the car, looked across its roof at his friend. He took a deep breath. "I don't care if it's like a blast furnace. This air is still cleaner and healthier than the shit most of the city folks in this country have to pull into their lungs."

"I'm glad you like it," Steve said as they walked toward the door of the cafe. "This is the atmosphere you'll be in for quite a while."

Track led the way into the cool interior. "Yeah," he said thoughtfully, "I haven't given much thought to how long this thing is going to take. Any estimates?"

They slid into a booth. Steve spoke in a whisper. "Hell, Dan, all we got to do is knock off or capture a hundred or so bad-asses. What do you think? A couple of weeks?"

"Try a couple of months," Track countered. "And that means if we survive that long we're sure winners. But that's the rub—surviving."

The waitress, a patient, matronly sort, took their orders. A couple of meals of eggs over easy, hash browns, sausage, toast and coffee don't take long to prepare. She was back with the food in ten minutes.

Steve swirled his toast in the yolk of his eggs. "When we get to Tucson, I want to stop at the airport and bus station."

"What for?" Track asked. "We leaving the car?"

"We sure are, but don't worry, we won't be walking," Steve answered. "That's where you'll stash your bags. I got some goodies waiting for you there."

"Goodies?"

"Yeah. Some stuff I 'organized.' Fatigues, load-carrying gear, boots, et cetera, et cetera."

"Tell me about the et ceteras."

"They're in the trunk of the Honda," Steve answered. "That's one reason I went to San Diego. I have a contact there."

"Contact for what?" Track asked.

"M-16s," Steve answered.

"Why that particular weapon?"

"Actually, I considered the old M-1 rifle," Steve said. "For open desert warfare, it's great—long-range accuracy, y'know."

"Yeah," Track agreed.

"Then I remembered the Caballo Mountains on the reservation," he continued. "Steep forested hills—close-in stuff. That made me think of Uzi submachine guns."

"So you figured M-16s were a compromise."

Steve shrugged and smiled. "Sure—plus the fact they were all I could get. Those and plenty of ammo."

"Anything heavier?"

"Sorry. No grenade launchers," Steve said. "No mortars, howitzers, tanks—"

"Okay," Track said.

"It's hard to arm yourself real exotically on such short notice," Steve said.

"Sure. I understand."

"I presume you got a personal piece," Steve said. "What is it?"

Track shrugged. "A 9 mm Beretta I carry around. I wasn't expecting any action of this magnitude." There was an accusing ring in his voice.

"There was no way to tell you anything, pal," Steve said, "I was under more surveillance than the *Playboy* centerfold of the month. And I wouldn't put it past Geronimo and his boys to use wiretaps despite their devotion to the ancient ways."

"I thought you called me from Tucson."

"I did. And at a public phone booth, too," Steve said. "To tell you the truth, I was so goosey after exfiltrating the reservation that I saw bad guys around every corner. I figured I was being followed or would be intercepted at any time."

"I'm not criticizing you," Track said, "but I wish you'd at least dropped me a hint."

"No way."

"Okay," Track said agreeably, "now let's get serious about how to pull this thing off. Last night in the hotel you spoke like you had some definite ideas."

"One definite idea," Steve corrected him. "And that is simply to get Geronimo Ferril and blow him and a couple of his hard-core followers away. That should end things right then and there."

"Don't you think there might be a new Geronimo?" Track asked. "Or a Natchez or Mangus Colorado or some other Apache leader?"

Steve shook his head. "Nope. The right moves on our part will create a real wide credibility gap for any future war chiefs and potential ghost dancers."

"You're probably right," Track said. "So what's the plan of action?"

Steve downed the last of his coffee and slid toward the edge of the booth. "It involves a long desert march to the objective and a sneak attack." He looked meaningfully at Track. "That's another bit of your expertise I need. I've seen your plans and concepts, Dan Track. You're the best damned S-3 I've ever known."

"I'm flattered," Track said. Then he spoke frankly. "But I'm a little disturbed you haven't planned anything beyond our infiltrating your war zone."

"What the hell? Even if I had, you'd just change everything around."

Track laughed a little. "Yeah. I guess I would."

"I'll explain more about the terrain of the operational area in the car."

"Great," Track said. He finished his coffee and followed Steve back to the car after paying for the bill.

THE STATE TROOPER turned his patrol car off the macadam and onto the dirt road leading into the interior of the Llanero Reservation. Pebbles banged against the bottom of the car as the tire treads grasped and flung them about, creating an uneven staccato.

The policeman could see occasional dwellings of the reservation's inhabitants spread along the small, shallow creek that flowed through their land. These were curious mixtures of the old and new. Wickiups complete with corrals holding horses were in evidence, while nearby sat modest but modern homes. Although there were a few outhouses, most of the residences were equipped with septic tanks which had been installed in connection with various government projects.

The building the law officer sought appeared in the near distance and he instinctively pressed down on the accelerator.

Another ten minutes of travel brought him to an open gate. He pulled through it and coasted the scant two dozen yards before stopping in front of his objective. The sign nailed above the doors and windows occupied the entire length of the building. It left no question as to the place's purpose—Llanero Apache Reservation Police.

Grabbing his small briefcase, the policeman left the car and quickly entered the building. He paused at the desk in the center of an outer office. A heavyset Apache, wearing the light blue of the local law, sat there. He didn't appear friendly.

The state trooper didn't know him. "How you doing?"

"Okay."

"Is Chief Aguila in?"

"Aguila ain't the chief no more and he sure as hell ain't in," the Apache said.

"What'd he do, move away?" the man asked, setting the briefcase on the desk.

"He got kicked off the force—drinking."

"Jesus, no shit?" The policeman pulled a neatly wrapped bundle of papers and handed them over. He eyed the other man. "I don't think we've met." He offered his hand. "My name is Turnbull."

The Indian shook Turnbull's hand, but said nothing.

Turnbull indicated the papers with a gesture. "The usual wanted posters and the latest reports and memoranda—the stuff that was designed to drive honest cops crazy."

"They'll be taken care of."

"Who's the new chief?"

"We ain't got nobody yet," the Indian cop said. He shoved the papers into one of his desk drawers and slammed it shut.

"Too bad about Steve," Turnbull said. "Hell, I've had a snort or two with him myself. He seemed to be able to handle the stuff okay."

"You know us Injuns," the Apache said sarcastically.

"I think I'll drop over and see him anyhow," the policeman said.

"He don't live here no more," the Indian said. "Moved to Phoenix. Anyhow, we don't want no outsiders roaming around. Things have changed around here."

Turnbull had sensed the hostility when he first arrived. "I can see they have. Well, when you get a new chief give him my best, huh? I'll see you with next month's paperwork."

"Okay."

Turnbull returned to his car. He backed around, then headed for the highway. "Damn!" he said aloud. Talking to himself was a habit he'd developed after years of solitary patroling in Arizona's wide-open, empty countryside. "Too bad about ol' Steve. He was a hell of a nice guy."

4

Once again Track and Steve Aguila were on the road. But this time they weren't enjoying the air-conditioned comfort of the rented Honda Accord. Instead they rode in a used Ford pickup. Fifteen years old, with smooth tires and a sun-faded rust-colored body, the old vehicle coughed along the highway. The burning hot, dry wind whipped in through the windows, baking the travelers' faces.

Dan Track and Steve Aguila looked a bit worse for wear. Battered straw Stetson-type hats, second-hand Levi's, bleached-out western-style cotton shirts and worn-down cowboy boots—all purchased at a Tucson Salvation Army store—gave them the appearance of a couple of Arizona citizens who had suffered a hell of a lot more bad luck than good lately, and hadn't been paid much for the inconvenience.

The gear stowed under the old tarp covering the truck bed would have belied the outward impression they presented to the world. The latest mountaineering and desert survival equipment, boots, desert camouflage fatigues, combat harness, M-16 rifles and plenty of ammo were securely hidden from view.

Track glanced around at the tattered interior of their humble conveyance. As usual, he was doing the driving. "I'm glad you didn't waste a lot of dough on our cover vehicle," he said, winking at Steve. "I wouldn't want folks to think we're putting on airs."

"We got to play the role," Steve insisted with a grin. "Anyhow, we're going to abandon this thing, and a fairly new pickup abandoned somewhere because of mechanical difficulty might really arouse somebody's curiosity. That's the last thing we want." Steve glanced over at him. "And you said we shouldn't try to hide this thing too well."

"If we made a serious attempt to hide this junker, and somebody stumbled across it, they'd sure as hell wonder why so much trouble had been taken to conceal such a pile of metal crap," Track said. "If we just park it alongside the road, it'll appear that it broke down and was left as useless by a couple of poor bastards who didn't have the dough or the inclination to get it fixed up."

"Sure," Steve agreed.

"And we'll make sure it won't start," Track added, "to hold the illusion. It would be just as suspicious as abandoning a new truck if somebody hops into this jalopy and fires her up without much trouble."

"You're a real smart cookie, Dan. Now you know why I asked you in on this thing," Steve said.

Their stopover in Tucson had been short but extremely busy. After arriving in the early evening, Steve had directed Track to drive south from the city to the airport. The first order of business was to return the automobile to the rental company. After settling the bill, the two men removed their luggage from the trunk and headed for the terminal.

A quick visit to the luggage lockers was all that was needed to grab a couple of large valises that Steve had stashed there. Track realized he was participating in a well-planned gathering of gear. The bags, while good sized, weren't large enough to contain all the equipment necessary for the undertaking. Track rightly figured there would be at least one more stop for supplies. But he wasn't sure if it would be at modern storage facilities or at a primitive, but well-concealed cache somewhere out in the desert. As they closed the locker doors, he whispered, "Where to next?"

"Bus station," Steve said.

"I've got an idea," Track said. "Let's cool it for a bit until a plane comes in. Then we can sort of melt into the crowd after they get their baggage. In case any of the gang from the reservation are waiting around to see if we show up, they might just miss us."

"Good idea," Steve said. "When we grab a cab, we'll be inconspicuous in the crowd."

"I also suggest we take separate taxis," Track added.

"You think on your feet, don't you?" Steve said.

"Just naturally sneaky," Track responded. "It's a trait that's kept me alive through several hairy situations."

"Yes," Steve agreed. "I've been in a couple of those with you, remember?"

"I sure do," Track acknowledged. "Now if you don't mind, let me know where we're going so I can end up at the same place you do."

Steve laughed. "The Greyhound Bus station."

On their way to the waiting area, Steve stopped and pointed to a copy of *People* magazine. On the cover was a photo of a pleasant-looking gentleman with gray hair. "That's Jerome Courtney," Steve said.

"Know him?" Track asked.

"Not really. But he's been a real champion of Indian rights."

Track nodded. "Oh, yeah. I've heard of him. A movie and TV producer, isn't he?"

"Right. A couple of his series are at the top of the Nielsen's," Steve said. "One hell of a man."

Track took one more look at the magazine then followed after Steve.

They took seats several yards apart. To the casual observer, they would appear to be nondescript, casually dressed travelers, not particularly excited about the trip they were about to take.

By sitting some distance apart, they were able to cover each other effectively in case something unexpected happened. Since Track was unknown in the area, it would probably be Steve who would draw any lethal attention.

A boring half hour crawled by before a sizable crowd appeared from the arrival area. Track and Steve quickly moved to the center of the crowd and walked slowly in the safety of the milling passengers until they got outside.

The cab rides were uneventful, and their arrival and brief visit to the bus depot produced more baggage. This time they took the stuff into the men's room and changed into the scruffy clothing that Steve had arranged for them.

Track stepped from the toilet stall and studied his reflection in the mirror. The fact that he hadn't shaved for forty-eight hours added to the illusion of tackiness and hard luck.

Steve joined him. He looked pointedly at Track's sprouting beard, then rubbed his own smooth face. "Sure glad we Indians don't have to put up with that inconvenience."

"Wait'll it really grows out," Track said with a wink. "You'll be shaking with envy."

"Not hardly," Steve said with a laugh. "Let's take our stuff outside. You wait there on the street with the gear. I'll be by within a half hour. I've got a beat-up old pickup waiting for me. I bought it before I left for San Diego. It's rusted out and has Arizona plates. The left front wheel doesn't have a hubcap."

"Right," Track said. He glanced around to make sure none of the other men in the rest room were close enough to hear. "Just for the hell of it, pop the horn three quick times when you pull up."

"Right," Steve agreed. "No horn means for you to cover my ass. Or haul it out, if there's somebody with me in the cab," Steve said. "We aren't expecting company."

"Okay. So, if you don't honk and I don't see anyone, I'll presume he's in the back of the truck."

"Or following," Steve added.

"When I start shooting, get out and run toward me," Track said. "I'll try real hard not to hit you."

"I'd appreciate that, pal," Steve said. "Let's move out."

Track's rendezvous with the truck had gone the easy way. Now the two friends continued south on State 83, heading for the other side of Fort Huachura southwest of the Dragoon Mountains—an area that had heard Apache war cries and gunshots in the past.

At that moment it appeared as if old times were back again.

TREVOR LEVANT GAZED from the large picture window to the smooth sand of the beach a hundred feet below. He lifted his eyes and enjoyed the sight of sailboats tacking back and forth in the gentle swells of the Pacific Ocean. Although Levant was slightly built and only five feet eight inches tall, his face appeared to have been chiseled from granite. The features were square and masculine, with heavy brows over eyes that masked their intellectual depth with a veneer of arrogance. His physical appearance gave the impression he was an aggressive individual with a natural instinct to be a leader.

Levant smiled to himself and raised the vodka martini to his lips for a quick sip. "I love the ocean."

"Oh, yeah?" His companion was a heavyset man with a dark scowl. Despite what was obviously an expensive suit, he looked rumpled and uncomfortable.

"I think it all comes from my New England background," Levant said. "My ancestors were whalers who sailed out of Massachusetts." He wore an expensive kimono of pure silk, its dark blue background festooned with delicate, yet boldly colorful flowers.

"Oh, yeah?"

Levant sneered. "Yeah. . . *yeah*!" He finished the drink and set it down on the table beside him. "You're a lousy conversationalist, Pugnaci."

"Right."

Levant shrugged. "But a hell of an organizer." The two men were in Levant's recreation room, his favorite part of the sprawling ranch-style home that looked down from the cliff to the ocean.

Expensive playthings were around the walls. The latest video games, an expensive dart set, a billiard table and a large, felt-covered poker table with built-in coasters and chip racks were part of the decor.

The house and grounds were in an isolated neighborhood a short distance from Newport Beach, California. Here were located the domiciles of some of California's wealthiest and most famous citizens.

"You want me to go on?" Pugnaci asked.

Levant fixed himself another drink. "Yes, of course. Pardon my silly attempts at interjecting anything so mundane as conversation into your disjointed mumblings."

"Right. Now should I go on?"

"Yes, please," Levant said with a sigh.

"Okay. The setup is solid now. Ferril's got everybody on the reservation either on his side or under control."

"What about that police chief or whatever he is?" Levant asked.

"You mean Aguila? He's gone. Probl'y lost in that desert out there," Pugnaci said. "Anyhow, nobody is worried about him. They figure he got hit in the ambush where they caught him and them last two Injun cops. Prob'ly crawled off somewhere to die."

"Prob'ly?" Levant asked sarcastically.

"Yeah, prob'ly," Pugnaci said, missing the tone in the other's voice. "Anyhow, they're looking around for him. If he shows up again, they'll blow his ass away good and proper."

Levant nodded. "Tell them to keep at it until they come up with the man—pardon the cliché—dead or alive."

"Right. Them Injuns will cough the guy up dead."

"Menacing, aren't they?"

"I ain't never seen a cold fish like that Ferril before in my life," Pugnaci said.

Levant raised his eyebrows. If Geronimo Ferril could impress a professional hit man like Pugnaci, he must be a force to be reckoned with. "Anything else happen?"

"They kilt a bunch o' Mezkins," Pugnaci said. "Three or four groups of 'em." He paused and frowned. "I don't like that much. It might bring somebody pokin' around."

Levant shook his head. "Hardly, my dear Pugnaci. Those are illegal aliens. When any appear on the reservation we have them removed for two reasons. First, and less important, it keeps the bloodlust alive and well in our savage friends; second, like members of all subcultures, these wetbacks and those who smuggle them in have an active and extensive grapevine established. When the word is passed that none are reappearing after entering the Llanero Reservation, they will avoid the place like the plague—again, pardon the cliché. Mexicans and Apaches have never been good friends. That will keep future interlopers at bay."

"Right."

"Thank you, Pugnaci," Levant sneered. "Thank you so much for that vote of confidence."

"Right."

"Anything else to add to your delightful report?"

"Ferril says the operation can start in another month."

"I trust his judgment implicitly," Levant said. "You may go now, Pugnaci. I wish to contemplate the sea."

"Right."

Levant waited until the large man had left the room before mixing another drink. He carried it to the window, and once again settled into a peaceful reverie.

The man who now placidly contemplated nature was born Trevor Morgan Levant into a wealthy New Bedford, Mass., family some thirty-five years previously. His parents, part of a merchant dynasty that had begun building its fortune in the shipping and whaling industries of the 1830s, had been brought together in a marriage that was as unquestionably arranged as it was accepted by the young couple. After all, they recognized themselves as part of a capitalist royalty, and they obeyed whatever fate was decreed for them with the same numb acceptance as had many princes and princesses in the Old World.

This unhappy union endured a quiet misery without the usual shouting and brawling of many lower-class mismatches. Mr. and Mrs. Levant appeared in public at the right times and in the right places, thus creating the illusion they were a normal, happily wed couple. They were so unremarkable in their feigned happiness that the news media soon ignored them altogether except on very special occasions.

The few sexual joinings, entered into with as much enthusiasm as their wedding by the couple, produced the desired heir. With that, Mr. and Mrs. Levant led separate lives, coming together only on required formal occasions or family gatherings, more for business than for any exchange of affection.

Young Trevor was raised by an army of servants, nannies, tutors and paid companions. Winters were spent in the family home in Apponagansett Bay, until he went away to school—an annual trek that began when he was six and continued well into his twenties—and he passed his summers on the family's private island nestled in the Muskeget Channel between Martha's Vineyard and Nantucket Island. This routine was broken by trips to Europe and an occasional junket to the Caribbean.

For the first twenty-two years of Trevor's life, it appeared as though he would be eased into the family's financial empire either in a managerial position if he was able, or in a phony executive posting where, if he proved talentless, he would have a fancy title but could do no real harm.

Trevor was to fit into neither of these categories.

Several sea captains were part of his ancestry, and it was from one of these stubborn and adventurous tyrants that Levant's cruel, hard-driving nature took him away from the peaceful ruthlessness of the wars of capitalism, and led him straight into the man-made hell of organized crime.

As a student at Amherst, Levant was one of the most enthusiastic to enter into the drug scene. At first he enjoyed the sensations of cocaine, and was moving rather smoothly into heroin when something inside his skull rang a bell. It happened during a sojourn in New York City where the high-powered "H" was more readily available. It was there that Levant saw his first real junkie—a street doper rather than the collegiate type who got high for kicks—and he realized the power behind drugs.

The stuff enslaved people, and those who controlled the substances had as much power over these unfortunates as any slave master. And the concept of having power over a group of strung-out serfs was pleasing to Levant.

He had already learned that money bought just about any damned thing a man could want: loyal followers, pseudo but acceptable friendships, grades. Also that it could smooth over many more of life's unexpected but inevitable moments of difficulty. Levant decided to sow his generous allowance into the rich soil of narcotics to see what he could reap.

By shrewd investments in merchandise, a sales staff and a cadre of enforcers, Levant was quickly able to set up an effective organization, which was returning his initial outlay a thousand percent per week.

He operated out of the fancy apartment his parents had leased for him—a Levant would not deign to live in a dormitory with the common herd. And the exclusivity of the neighborhood kept the cops off his ass and out of his inventory.

Then he took a fall.

Even the Levant money couldn't help after a whopping sale to an undercover narc. The entrepreneur of drugs ended up in front of a stern judge who socked him with a staggering ten-year prison term in the Massachusetts state slammer.

Then the family fortune came in handy.

Appeals, hearings and petitions bombarded the legal system. Levant did his part by being a model prisoner and staying out of trouble. The combination of these efforts brought about his release in three years. Part of the parole stipulation was that he get out of Massachusetts and stay out.

Levant thought this unreasonable, but it would not have mattered anyway. His own family had come to that same conclusion. They thought if they sent him to college in a state far away from the temptations of civilization's flesh-and-dope pots, he would straighten up and in time be worthy of once again belonging to their exclusive clan.

By upper-class New England thinking, Arizona is a wild, desolate and empty pile of sand full of cowboys, Indians and lizards. The Levant family pictured Phoenix as a small desert town of plank and adobe buildings. When they learned that Arizona State University was located at that particular place, they packed Levant off to finish his education there—though they really didn't expect he'd get much of one.

Levant, to his own surprise, found himself enrolled in a first-rate institution of higher education. Trapped into a no-nonsense curriculum as a history major, and with seven more years in state prison waiting for him if he screwed up, the young man applied himself diligently and wholeheartedly. He even lived in the dorm.

And that's where he met Geronimo Ferril.

This man, a few years older than Levant, was attending school through a grant from the federal government. A full-blooded Apache Indian, Ferril was an anthropology student with a special interest in Indians of the American Southwest—particularly his own tribe.

His research, which had gone on for six years, included field trips and an extensive study of all dialects of the Apache people. Using a tape recorder and an old dictionary written by a long-forgotten missionary who had lived among these Indians, Ferril became an unheralded but thoroughly expert linguist in several Apache languages—particularly that of his own little-known Llanero tribe.

Levant and Ferril became roommates in the dormitory. Although no deep friendship was formed, the two sensed they were kindred souls, drifting through a world they would love to take advantage of. Such rapport and understanding are the things from which serious partnerships evolve.

Levant learned his new friend had been raised in grinding indigence in a seesaw life that kept him on both sides of the border between the State of Arizona and the *Republica de Mexico*. Levant thought this rather interesting. Then when Ferril told him of smuggling dope into the U.S. as a youngster to make money, the college-boy ex-convict suddenly found his roommate absolutely fascinating.

And Levant was soon back at his old games.

Unfortunately for Levant, the U.S. Customs were a tough bunch of dedicated lawmen, and they kept a keen eye on activities along the international border. This made peddling dope much tougher in Arizona than it had been in Massachusetts. One dreary evening, after an intercepting raid by the border patrol had resulted in his losing a particularly large shipment, Levant was bemoaning the situation to a sympathetic Ferril. It was out of this conversation that a grandiose scheme was set up in which the Llanero reservation, whose acreage ran to the Mexican border, could be made into a large safe area.

The casual chitchat had grown into a serious conspiracy in which Levant supplied the money while Ferril supplied the historical and ethnic know-how. The execution of the plan had begun with Ferril appearing among the Llanero Apaches preaching to them of ghost dances.

Levant turned from the window to mix himself one more drink when the phone rang. He waited for his houseboy to appear and announce that the call was for him. Levant walked to the corner table and picked up the telephone. "Yes?"

"Trevor, this is Jerome Courtney. I just wanted to let you be the first to know that the television special we've worked so hard for is now officially scheduled for next week."

"How wonderful!" Levant exclaimed. "I'm delighted—and I imagine you are too, Jerry."

"Certainly," Courtney said. "And we owe it all to you, Trevor. Without your support and untiring efforts this program would never have gotten off the ground. It's going to help a lot of American Indians, believe me."

"That's exactly what we wanted," Levant said. "And don't you be so modest. As president of the Committee for Advancement of Native Americans, you certainly did your part."

"I've been so busy with my latest picture that I don't feel I've really pulled my weight. But thank you just the same," Courtney said. "However, that project is over and done with now, completely freeing me up. But the real exciting part of the special is that there'll be plenty of celebrities in attendance. We know we can count on Marlon Brando, Jane Fonda and a few others."

Levant recalled Brando's past support for efforts directed against injustices to Indians. "He's just who we need."

"We've also many special acts lined up," Courtney continued.

"I was afraid we wouldn't have time to get them together."

"Just about everyone in show business has skits or songs they can perform at the drop of a hat," Courtney assured him. "And we've signed several of the best and most popular."

"Are there any from your television shows?" Levant asked.

Courtney laughed. "Just let me say that it doesn't hurt to be a producer."

"I suppose not! And I'm so deeply, deeply moved," Levant said in an emotional tone.

"And I am too, Trevor. Well, I must go now. There's a million things to do, but I did most certainly want you to know of these latest, most wonderful events."

"Thank you for calling," Levant said. "Goodbye, Jerry."

He hung up the phone and went back to mix the drink. When he was finished he suddenly laughed and held the glass aloft in a sardonic toast. He spoke in an imitation John Wayne voice: "Here's to all them pesky Redskins!"

5

Track, barely breathing, knelt with one knee digging into the sandy soil. His eyes and ears were atuned to the desert sounds with the intensity of a hunting hawk. The moon was fiendishly bright, casting a yellowish glare that was concentrated by the whiteness of the sandy terrain. Ahead of him, also in a watchful position, Steve Aguila surveyed the area around them.

Both men wore fatigues splotched with a brown and tan camouflage pattern. Their short-brimmed hats, turned up at the front to offer better visibility, were of the same material and colors. Their combat harnesses, a combination of web belt, pouches and a small back pack supported over their shoulders by nylon suspenders, were compactly and efficiently packed with ammo, LRP rations, a change of clothing and other personal essentials. It was a tribute to their skills that they were able to move reasonably quietly while loaded down with so much gear.

Each man also carried four canteens. The two attached to carrying straps on the backpack were of one-quart capacity, and the other pair held two quarts. Although Steve had given assurances that the base camp had its own good water supply, there was always a chance they would be separated from that area for long periods of time. In the Arizona desert, without water, a man's body could dehydrate to the point of death within twenty-four hours. Thus, H_2O was as precious to them as their life's blood.

One big problem was Track's boots. Although of good-quality leather and nylon, they had only recently been purchased by Steve for this operation. Due to the unusual circumstances and the time frame they were locked into, Track had been forced to break a cardinal rule of soldierly good sense: Never go out into the field in stiff, brand-new footgear. But Track had not known what he was headed for when he left Albuquerque to meet Steve in San Diego. Several pairs of well-fitting, perfectly broken-in boots sat in a closet back at his house.

Track shifted slightly and grimaced at the pain where his feet were being rubbed by the rigid leather. He caught Steve's signal ahead, and got slowly to his feet. Once moving, he forgot about the discomfort as all of his senses were returned to a heightened awareness of the surroundings.

They were moving through unfriendly territory. Before the meeting in San Diego, Steve had gone through hell during his break for safety from the Llanero Reservation. Forced into a hasty withdrawal, he had been ill equipped, with a single canteen, low-quarter police shoes, and a patrolman's uniform. The Apache had traveled slowly and with a great deal of thirst while his trail was dogged by persistent pursuers. Only great skill, born of his natural instincts, combined with solid Special Forces training had brought him through it.

Steve's basic plan of action would come to an end shortly. Their destination was a private hideaway of his, up in the Caballo Mountains of the Llanero Reservation. Once there, Dan Track would take over and direct their two-man operation against the enigmatic Geronimo Ferril who had to be eliminated before the Apaches living there returned to normal lives.

Steve's unerring trek took them to the northeast, toward the dark humps of the Caballos which were linked to the Dragoon Mountains through subterranean rock formations that hadn't seen the light of day nor felt a fresh breath of wind for more than ten thousand years.

The desert vegetation, while scrubby and only waist high, grew thicker. It was a mixed blessing. While it afforded the two infiltrators better cover, it also increased the noise they made in spite of the skill and patience they practiced. It also meant that any potential bushwhackers would also find it easier to conceal themselves.

Track closed the distance between himself and his friend. The necessity for space between them decreased with this more abundant cover. Steve again signaled then dropped to a kneeling position. Track followed suit. This was no cause for alarm. Moving through the enemy like this required that they stop and remain absolutely still and silent on occasion. It gave them the opportunity to observe their perilous environment, and if an unfriendly type heard any accidental noise they might make, he would dismiss it on not hearing a second one. With luck, the man would conclude that his imagination was running wild or that some animal or bird had disturbed the silence of the night.

After ten minutes Steve's barely discernible form straightened up into the murkiness. A subtle wave of his arm signaled them forward, and the two continued their slow, near-silent movement through the manzanita and cactus.

The moon followed its natural arc to drift across the wide sky as the journey continued unabated except for the stops for observation. The big heat of summer had yet to come; it was early in the season. Although the days were hot, the night's chill at that time of the year made moving a welcome way to get the blood circulating and flowing back into near-frozen hands and feet. The crisp, clean air provided another benefit, too. Its invigorating freshness kept away the fatigue that could sap a man's strength and alertness. But even with all that, Geronimo Ferril could field dedicated men skillful in war's deadly arts. Even the most alert infiltrators could walk into situations of great peril.

The ambush hit them at a little past one o'clock in the morning.

An explosion of small-arms fire and the resultant flashes of muzzle blast turned the area into an arena of hell. Track swung the M-16 in an instinctive arc, pumping the trigger to throw out a maximum number of bullets.

In the blinking brightness of muzzle blasts, he could see an Apache warrior, his long hair flying, slammed back by the fusillade. Track ran past him, pressing toward Steve, who was also hauling ass and laying out a curtain of 5.56 mm slugs toward the ambushers.

Track, knowing they were moving through the first echelon of potential killers, flipped the selector switch to full-auto and swung his weapon in the opposite direction. He kicked off small-fire bursts to his right front. A hidden warrior, half his face blown away leaving a hideous red gap, appeared to leap from the cover of darkness and vegetation before collapsing back to the ground.

Steve, still in the lead, had sensed that Track had changed his field of fire. With the same instinct that had served them both in Vietnam, he continued to cover the left side of the firefight.

Yells, screams and blasting weapons continued unabated. Track, however, was able to make himself heard above the bedlam of the battle. "We're through 'em!" he shouted. "Turn and stand!"

"Roger!" Steve bellowed back. He dropped and whirled toward their rear at the same time. Track moved off to the right another five yards until he was even with him, then also turned to face the now broken ambush formation. Together they fired in overlapping arcs at the Indians who now were forced to move toward them to continue what they had started.

One warrior, screaming in a hideous soprano, managed to slip through the hail of steel, and closed with Track. Track, reaching the end of a magazine at that time, heard the mechanism of his weapon lock on the empty chamber. He rose and struck out with a horizontal butt stroke.

The Indian's momentum carried him past the most lethal part of the blow and he only caught a piece of the inner stock above the ear. He crashed into Track and both went down rolling and kicking to the sand. Track's M-16 went whirling off to one side, but his right hand, now free, dug into the nylon holster on the web suspenders and came out holding the Beretta.

The 9 mm barked twice, each cough heralding a slug that struck the Apache's face. He twisted sideways and dropped like a sack of grain.

Track, not wasting a motion, aimed the pistol toward the other attackers. He continued to fire. After squeezing off three more rounds, he could see the fight was over.

Steve, as soaked in sweat as Track, stood breathing laboriously with the effort he had just expended. Then he grinned over at him. "I told you these were some real badass dudes."

"You're a master of understatement." Track walked over and picked up his M-16. "That first guy gave his buddies away. He either misunderstood the ambush plans or got excited and fired too quickly."

"He probably just lost his head," Steve said. "That's always been a problem with us—more warriors than soldiers."

"Something like that could fuck up a train wreck," Track said. He glanced out into the night. "How much farther is this mountain stronghold of yours?"

"In miles or hours?" Steve asked.

"In ambushes," Track answered.

"You'll have to ask Geronimo Ferril that," Steve said. He glanced at the dead men, surprised to see there were only five. "A couple of minutes ago I would have sworn there were two dozen of those bastards."

"If that's what it's like to fight a quintet of Apaches, I can't wait to take on a hundred or so," Track said.

"My people have never been known as shrinking violets," Steve said matter-of-factly.

Track nodded his agreement then motioned toward the distant mountains. "After you."

"You're too kind," Steve said.

The duo once again moved out, closing with whatever fate the fickle gods of war had ordained for them.

6

Geronimo Ferril opened his eyes slowly, letting his waking mind ease into awareness of his surroundings.

The interior of the wickiup was slightly smokey. The rising sun shining in through the blanketed entrance created shafts of haze in the lodge. Ferril turned his head and glanced at the girl beside him. Her long, raven-colored hair was disheveled, lying across her face, puffy with sleep. She wore no makeup, yet she radiated a primitive beauty that could never be matched by the modern world's cosmetics or fashions.

Ferril felt the same stirrings that had driven him to take her three times the night before. The second time had been when he'd been awakened by an abrupt explosion of gunfire. The disturbance hadn't alarmed him, however, for he knew there would be scouts sent out to investigate. They would report to him as quickly as possible.

Now he reached under the blanket and placed his hand over a breast, softly manipulating the fleshy mound. The young woman, his wife, stirred. Her eyes opened slightly, then she closed them again.

He grasped her shoulder and rolled her over on her back. The girl, now awakening, offered no resistance, and lay silently letting him have his way. When he finished, Ferril lay on top of her for several more moments, then wordlessly threw the blanket aside and stood up. After giving her nakedness a casual scrutiny to enjoy a better look at what had given him so much pleasure, he went over to his pile of clothes and picked up the breechcloth. He adjusted it around his waist and under his crotch. He ignored the shirt, leaving it on the earthen floor as he donned the deerskin moccasins and headband. Then he stepped outside into the fresh light of dawn.

Geronimo Ferril, Ph.D., stood in his primitive dress, the perfect picture of the stone-age man, yet possessing the penetrating mental strength of a true intellectual. Other people now emerged from their dwellings. They raised their hands in greeting to him. He returned the salutations, then after several deep breaths, began his morning ritual of a five-mile, non-stop, rapid run. This was done in a circuit that carried him around the camp of some six hundred souls—two hundred of whom were warriors.

He ran effortlessly, tirelessly and with no conscious pain or discomfort despite the demands he placed on his middle-aged body. Powerfully built, his muscular legs pumped mechanically as if the man was a perpetual-motion machine in which each movement gave momentum to the next in ever-expanding bursts of energy.

This disregard of physical pain had been developed during the twenty years he had devoted to the study of ancient Indian religion and custom. His first exposure to this historic phenomenon had been as disrespectful and casual as the white students'. But the deeper he sank into the meditative oneness with nature practiced by his ancestors, the more he realized they had achieved mind over matter in a more superior way than whites or even Orientals.

Indian warriors in various cultures purposely endured great periods of torture and deprivation to increase their spiritual strength, a strength that inevitably flowed into the physical side of their beings. Inserting sharpened bones into pectoral muscles and hanging from rawhide ropes tied to the tops of lodges for days was one supreme test of a people who equated the word "manhood" with *warriorhood*. A man was either a warrior or he was below contempt. Those who failed these terrible tests were cruelly ostracized. In some tribes, they were even forced to wear women's clothing.

Geronimo Ferril's attachment to the old ways began as a thin thread, which grew in strength until it finally drew him back to what the Great Spirit of All Indians had meant him and all his race to be.

Two wicked-looking scars on each side of Ferril's chest attested to his own passing back into the old ways. This ritual had led to a more subtle penetration of the ancient customs. He found himself strangely drawn to the old gods despite the cold, clear logic his education had forced upon his mental processes. The nights he spent alone on the Llanero Reservation during study trips drew him closer to these deities. It seemed as though they whispered to him while he slept. But, oddly, it was when he was back in his offices at Arizona State that the one impelling thing occurred that would drive him back to the old ways.

It began with a study of an Apache named Nakaidoklini.

Nakaidoklini, in June 1881, brought the ghost dance to the White Mountain Apaches. He spoke of the resurrection of the dead through these unusual dances and ceremonies. The attempt came to nothing, however, when an Indian agent named J.C. Tiffany became alarmed at what he considered a sinister activity. He informed the army, and a detachment of troops arrived on the scene and took Nakaidoklini into custody.

A rescue attempt by the Apaches proved disastrous. In the ensuing fight, the soldiers killed the prophet, then managed to barely escape to the safety of Fort Apache.

Geronimo Ferril felt a strong attachment to Nakaidoklini. Like himself, this medicine man had been educated by the whites. It was only after attending a Christian school in Santa Fe, New Mexico, that Nakaidoklini had returned to his people. At that time he began the ghost dance to bring all the Apaches who had ever walked the earth back from the Spirit World to soundly defeat the white men and drive them from these lands forever.

The influence of that phase of history was so strong on Geronimo Ferril that sometimes he truly felt he was Nakai-doklini reincarnated, or that the old prophet's spirit was speaking to him from the darkness of death.

There was no doubt in his mind that the idea of the ghost dance would appeal to modern Apaches. They were fed up with the shoddy treatment they'd received over the decades. Being warlike by nature, most would love a chance to escape the yoke of the Bureau of Indian Affairs.

Ferril was sure of himself in beginning the ghost dance, but intellectually, he realized he must consider what would happen once the movement caught on. There was even a chance of independence for the Llaneros if the right people could be brought in to back them up. And there were plenty of celebrities and other influencial people who opposed the mistreatment of Native Americans as much as the Indians themselves did.

The unexpected business proposition from Trevor Levant proved to be the exact thing he needed. Ferril had been involved in drug smuggling himself before his student days, and he realized the staggering amounts of money that could be made in it. With the proper influence and enough money, anything was possible. Though he still walked the white man's road in at least half his life, this scheme that he and Trevor Levant were working on went much further than Levant realized. It was Ferril's dream to eventually turn the Llanero Apache Reservation into the Llanero Apache Nation.

His final plans for this Native American country were not all that original. He saw himself as a religious leader not unlike the Ayatollah Khomeini in Iran, and the economy of his new nation not unlike that of Colombia in South America—based on narcotics.

Ferril made his last turn and headed back toward the village. He ran with the same freshness and cadence as when he had started. His breathing was deep but regular, and his legs, corded with bulging muscle and veins, continued to carry him effortlessly.

As he drew closer to the wickiups, he could see a group of people gathering around his dwelling. Though sensing trouble, he did not hurry his pace. He ran around the edge of the camp, then turned in and went directly to where several dozens of people were waiting for him. Somewhere, in another part of the encampment, he could hear weeping women.

Ferril's woman, who had gotten up and prepared his meal after he had left the wickiup, gave him a shirt and went back to her tasks. Lobo, one of the young men he had chosen as a war chief, waited until Ferril had slipped into the garment before he spoke.

"We have problems, Geronimo." He pronounced the word Hay-Ro-Nee-Mo in the proper manner. Many of the Llaneros had used English so long that they mispronounced even their own names.

"What is it?" Ferril asked.

"Five men were killed last night," Lobo said. "We found them down in the scrub south of the mountains." He paused. "I'm sorry." Lobo, a marine veteran who had served in Vietnam, was in charge of the net of ambushes set to catch any interlopers or defectors.

Geronimo Ferril's face was impassive, but an anger seethed beneath the surface of his cool exterior. "Aguila?"

"I think so," Lobo answered. "But there were two guys—each wearing jungle boots. One was a big dude, probably a white." He held up a shell casing. "Looks like M-16s. There were also a couple of 9 mm. Probably a Browning or Beretta or maybe even a Luger."

"What about our own men? Did they appear to have given a good account of themselves?"

Lobo hesitated. "Well . . . yeah, I guess so. They sure as hell fired a lot of rounds."

"How did it appear the ambush went down?" Geronimo asked.

"Somebody fucked up," Lobo answered. "The two dudes had walked right into it, then one of our guys cut loose before they were deep enough into the position."

"Goddamn it!" Geronimo looked at the others. "I keep telling you that there were two principal things that brought about our people's defeat in the last century. The first was our sparse population. The Indian birthrate could not match the replacement depots of even a small professional army like the whites had in those days. They overwhelmed us. The second, and most disgraceful, contribution to our downfall was our lack of discipline. The best thought-out plans and strategies would go to hell because some knucklehead would get so excited he couldn't contain himself and he'd move too soon or too quick and blow the situation wide open."

The others, though not participants in either the old Apaches' defeat or the blown ambush of the previous night, hung their heads nevertheless.

"Five good men were blown away because some asshole lost his head." He paused to let the sound of the wailing women be heard. "You want your wives and girlfriends to have to go through that for no good reason?" He paused and let the words sink in. "That son of a bitch Aguila, who evidently now has somebody else with him, is loose somewhere, armed to the teeth. He must be found and taken out. It could have happened last night, except for one fuck-up." He scowled. "Let's get some more war parties out and see what we can dig up. Maybe with a little luck, we'll be able to track the two down."

Lobo yelled out some orders and the men immediately began to assemble into their combat units. Geronimo watched them for a moment, then turned and went inside to do his own thinking on the subject.

STEVE AGUILA'S STRONGHOLD was an oasis in comparison to the desert below. The lowlands of the reservation, which comprised the greatest percentage of the area, were barren rocky desert. But here, high in the Caballo Mountains, a lush forest and grasslands existed, the greenery fed by underground streams. The largest of these formed a small river that flowed down to the flatlands. It was just a small creek by the time it reached the desert, but it provided an oblong oasis around which the Apaches could raise a few sheep and livestock for their own use.

The mountainous terrain was so steep that normal habitation was impossible. But Steve Aguila, as a young boy, had found a small meadow on a plateau that was hidden from view by trees. Although the meadow was only twenty yards across, a small spring bubbled up from the ground sending its precious water flowing no more than a short distance before it soaked back into the soil. Here, as a boy and later as a young man, he came to get away from the miserable existence of the reservation Indian. It was his secret, something he refused to share with anyone else. Even his best friends were puzzled about where he went to hide, and they spent many hours searching for him. But none had ventured through the thick rocky outcrop with the hidden opening that led to the meadow.

It was midmorning as Dan Track sat with his blistered feet now treated and healing. He looked at the Band-Aids covering the sensitive areas. "At least those boots are broken in now."

"Yeah," Steve Aguila remarked. "You won't have to go throught that again."

Track was doing more than just relaxing on the soft, grassy earth. His attention was on the highly detailed topographic map Steve had provided him with. A steady hour of this paper reconnaissance had made him as familiar with the layout of the reservation as Steve was. The only difference was that, despite the accurate contour lines and elevation indicators, Dan didn't have a real feel for the land or its dips, vegetation or other characteristics. Only a physical scouting expedition could reveal those secrets.

Steve watched him intently. "Well? What do you think?"

"All the permanent buildings seem located along the creek," Track said. "Any temporary dwellings that might not be on the map?"

"Oh, yeah," Steve said, "and they're moved around all the time. There's always some guy that gets pissed off at his neighbors or just wants to be alone for a while. He'll go off and build a wickiup off in the desert somewhere."

"What does he do for water?"

"We all have pickups," Steve explained. "The guy'll drive back and forth between his little camp and the creek with jerry cans."

"In other words, we might run into somebody just about any place out here, huh?"

Steve shrugged. "I didn't say it'd be easy."

Track put the map down. He poured some of the boiling water from the pot nestled in the campfire into a canteen cup. "We'll have to go on an old-fashioned recon patrol." He mixed some instant coffee in the metal container.

"Right," Steve said. "Maybe we can get Ferril at the same time."

"When I say 'recon,' I mean it in the purest sense," Track said.

"By the book? No combat no matter what?"

"Exactly," Track said. "I want to avoid any open contact at this time until we get our bearings."

"We've already had some open contact."

"Okay," Track conceded. "But our staying out of touch now will make 'em that much more nervous."

"Sounds reasonable," Steve remarked. "To tell you the truth, I don't know which of those wickiups belongs to Geronimo or any of his war chiefs anyhow."

"That's what the recon is for," Track said. "We'll have to find a good observation point and spend some time watching what's going on."

"Cover is sparse in that area," Steve warned him.

Track shrugged. "Well, pal, as you said—you never promised this would be easy."

"Yeah," Steve said. "I hate like hell to sound ominous, but there's an old Apache war saying that's been running through my head over and over since last night."

"What's that?" Track asked.

"It's a good day to die."

7

The line of limousines stretched back a half-dozen blocks onto Santa Monica Boulevard from the entrance into Century Plaza. The canopied area in which the sedate Cadillacs, Rolls Royces and Mercedeses discharged their passengers was a narrow gap on the sidewalk surrounded by a pressing, cheering crowd of movie and TV fans.

The star-studded event had been heralded for weeks on television, in print and even on billboards. Jerome Courtney's publicity department had gone into high gear, bombarding the public so that even the most conservative of experts predicted no less than eighty-five percent of American TV sets would be tuned that night to this live special, entitled simply "The Hour of Native Americans."

Three sweeping searchlights shot their wide beams into the starry California darkness overhead. Dozens of cameramen and reporters representing local Los Angeles, the three major networks and several foreign TV organizations, jostled for position in the street.

Camera shots panned into each other and microphone cords intertwined as the frenzy to get good shots of celebrities and exclusive interviews continued unabated.

The famous people smiled as they climbed gracefully from the limousines. They all paused to wave to the crowd. Charming and fantastic in looks, dress and demeanor, they displayed their attractiveness to full advantage, knowing just how long to maintain a pose before moving on to the entrance of the studios.

An enterprising reporter from one of the Los Angeles independent stations scored big by maneuvering a famous young TV series star into a position between himself and the barricade that held back the crowd. Myra Hawkins, though relatively new to stardom and its tedious obligations, feinted and dodged rather expertly in the cover of her male escort, but it was to no avail. Hemmed in, she controlled her irritation and smiled widely into the camera lens, bringing her acting talents to the fore as she appeared to be "totally delighted" to submit to a short interview. "Ms Hawkins!" the reporter said loudly over the noise of the crowd, "the fans, and indeed, the home audience are so moved by the unselfish devotion of not only yourself but of many of your colleagues in the entertainment industry in dedicating yourselves to this most worthwhile of causes, the plight of the American Indian."

"Thank you," said Ms Hawkins. "I feel compelled to lend my support to the Committee to Advance Indians."

"That's the Committee to Advance Native American Causes," the reporter quickly corrected her.

"Yes," she said keeping the smile wide and glittering without the slightest relaxation of her facial muscles.

"Last year you took a break from your series to star in Jerome Courtney's movie *Cheyenne Lament* in which you played a young Indian woman of the 1890s. Did that in any way influence you to be here tonight?"

"Oh, yes," Ms Hawkins responded with a serious nod of her elaborately coiffured head. "That role brought me to the realization of the terrible things that have been done to our Indians. I didn't *play* the part of Little Deer, I *lived* it!"

"I'm sure you did, Ms Hawkins. Your performance was simply wonderful. How—"

She impatiently continued her speech. "When an actress—a real actress—plays a part, she totally lets the character absorb her. I became Little Deer, the Cheyenne woman. I shared her feelings, her anguish, her loves, even her terror."

"And you were most believable," the reporter said.

"Thank you so much." Ms Hawkins smiled. "There's nothing—absolutely nothing—I wouldn't do to aid and encourage this worthwhile cause."

Her escort, a studio publicist, quickly stepped in. "Ms Hawkins is totally dedicated to the Committee to Advance Native American Causes. When Mr. Courtney asked her to be here tonight she was delighted to attend."

"Of course I was! I'm terribly, terribly involved, y'know." Before she could say more she was pulled away toward the entrance.

The reporter, now facing the camera alone, fell back into his standby patter. "That was Myra Hawkins, ladies and gentlemen, another of Hollywood's famous people who are attending this television special designed to bring public attention to the unfortunate conditions that exist on America's Indian reservations." As he spoke, his eyes scanned the arriving celebrities for another interview.

Inside the Century Plaza Studios, in a room off the main broadcasting stage, Jerome Courtney looked from the TV set he had been monitoring to Trevor Levant standing beside him.

"Most fortunate," Courtney remarked. The two had been switching from channel to channel checking out the live coverage of the night's event. He and Courtney had just witnessed Ms Hawkins's response to the reporter's questions. "Myra is becoming quite good at dealing with the press. Frankly, I was a bit worried about her."

Trevor Levant was also pleased. "It did go quite well," he agreed. "Perhaps Brando or Fonda or Spacek would have been a bit smoother, but I think Myra Hawkins was more than adequate."

"Yes," Courtney said. Then he laughed softly. "She's really quite intelligent for one of Hollywood's Miss Big Tits."

"Don't worry," Levant said. "Even if she had committed some small *faux pas*, it wouldn't have mattered. There's enough of the really big people here to have made up for it."

"As it is, things look even better," Courtney said happily.

"You've drawn yourself into this very deeply," Levant said. "You really care, Jerry, and your emotional commitment tonight is total."

Courtney nodded. "Yes." He laid a hand on Levant's shoulder. "And so is yours, Trevor. I'm so appreciative of all your support."

"Then let's turn our attention to the job at hand, shall we?"

"An excellent suggestion," Courtney said. He switched off the TV. "From this point on, the show is totally in the hands of the director and his staff. We've nothing to do but sit tight and wait for our cues."

The two settled down on the large sofa in the dressing room they had been assigned. Outside, in the wings, the various acts due on first were nervously waiting. Other performers, scheduled to appear later, rested in their dressing rooms. Some caught quick naps to fight their nerves, but a couple of the older actors revived their professional confidence with bourbon and Scotch, while the more uneasy of the younger set smoked joints or snorted coke to bolster their self-assurance.

The studio was beginning to fill up. Rather than having auditorium-type seating, it had been decided to create the appearance of a cabaret. The audience would be at tables, not in rows of seats. To add to the illusion, champagne and white wine were available, sweating in buckets of ice.

Previously stationed TV cameras were making test shots for the control booth located directly above them. Camera directors spoke into microphones to give the camera operators their final instructions.

Harried ushers, well-rehearsed and experienced, worked in controlled panic as they made sure each and every arriving celebrity couple was seated at the correct table according to their current popularity and stardom. Rank has its privileges in the entertainment industry no less than the military, and those stars at the pinnacle of success at that particular moment would have the best and most visible seats.

At the appointed time the director gave the word electronically from the control booth, and suddenly it was show time!

Camera lights glowed, music burst forth from the orchestra, and the host, a stand-up comedian now making it big in a sitcom, was introduced. He opened with a few jokes, then introduced the first guest star, a diminutive woman singer whose booming voice belied her size.

The next two hours passed with more acts and commercials, interspersed with short tapes on conditions of various Indian reservations and the usual obligatory shots of the stars in the audience. Forewarned, they had already posed showing smiles and expressions of concern and devotion.

At the midpoint of the show, just after the station-identification break, the host reappeared at the modernistic, plastic podium provided for him. He acknowledged this fresh explosion of applause as he did all others, with a humble bow of his head.

"Ladies and gentlemen, this television special—a most worthy one—is the result of countless hours of sacrifice and devotion by one man, a man who has spent more than half his life laboring for the rights of Native Americans. He has enjoyed great professional success and the monetary rewards that went with it, yet he never forgot the cause that has remained so deeply a part of him. It gives me great pleasure to introduce the eminent producer of both film and television drama, Mr. Jerome Courtney."

Courtney, dignified in his tuxedo, came out from the wings and walked to the podium. He and the comedian exchanged embraces, then the host stepped back discreetly beyond camera range while Courtney faced the audience, and the standing ovation given him. It lasted a full minute before the floor director signaled to the audience and they gradually slowed the clapping and resumed their seats.

"Thank you. Thank you so much," Courtney said. "This evening's activities are the culmination of a lifelong dream of mine. This is a start—just a start—of a major campaign in which serious wrongs that have gone on for several generations will be brought to a final and quick halt.

"Life on the Indian reservations is something with which the average American has only a passing acquaintance. It is my purpose now to raise the public's consciousness of the injustices and mistreatment that threaten the Indian's dignity as well as his physical well-being. Rather than cover all the reservations, I am going to concentrate on one, emphasizing that what you are about to see is typical."

He paused, his face serious. "Ladies and gentlemen, I am about to take you, via tape, on a tour of the Llanero Apache Reservation in Arizona."

Busy hands hit switches as the image of Jerome Courtney faded out, and a picture of rocky desert, studded with cactus, slowly shimmered into focus.

The tape ran only for ten minutes, but the chief film editor of Courtney's organization had skillfully blended cuts of crude wickiups, dry wells, poor medical facilities, and scraggly, inferior-looking stock, so that the aura of defeat and hopelessness was pervasive.

When the tape ended a compulsory commercial extolling the virtues of one soft drink over the other via a taste test was shown before Jerome Courtney made another appearance.

"Thus, ladies and gentlemen, you can see our task is a hard one. It will take new laws, more efforts and an awakening of national morals to right these wrongs. Tonight is a beginning. You, I . . . we all, now know the truths of these conditions. You may ask how you can help. The first thing to do is write your congressional representatives—indeed, the president—and let them know of your indignation, and demand that the government live up to the treaties and agreements made with these tribes. Where there are past injustices, change them! Where there are potential ones, prevent them! The American Indians' suffering is your suffering, for it reflects on you. The next thing you can do is—pardon this crude gambling colloquialism, but—put your money where your mouth is. Send whatever you can afford to CANAC—the Committee to Advance Native American Causes. There will be more details at the end of the show. Thank you. Thank you very much."

Courtney bowed to the standing ovation. Again, time was of the essence, and the floor director did his job by bringing the host back and signaling both Courtney and the audience that any more ovations would cause the show to run over.

Trevor Levant, waiting in the wings, offered his hand as Courtney rejoined him. "Well done, Jerry! I'm very proud of you."

Courtney took a deep breath. He was very emotional about the cause. The control he had exhibited before the cameras was gone for a few moments. He gradually regained his usual composure. "Thank you, Trevor. I wish you could have been out there with me."

Levant held up his hand. "Oh, no! I can't stand to be in front of an audience. I would have made a fool of myself and set us back twenty years."

"I doubt that very much," Courtney said. "You've done so much, and given so much time and money. Surely you could forgo your shyness so that at least you could serve as a good example."

Levant shook his head. "I couldn't possibly."

"Very well," Courtney said. "How about your picture in one of our magazine or newspaper ads?"

"Not even there."

"But, surely, since you've become the executive secretary of CANAC, you wouldn't object to that."

But Levant was adamant. "I'm afraid, dear Jerry, that such publicity would force me to withdraw. I cannot stand it. I fear I suffer from a personality maladjustment. I am simply unable to tolerate such situations. Please understand."

Courtney smiled. "Of course, my friend. I'm sorry if I'm being pushy. It's just that I'm so damn grateful."

"Then that's enough for me," Levant said.

The two walked back to the dressing room. They had just settled down to watch the closing of the show when an usher knocked lightly on the door and leaned inside. "Telephone call for Mr. Levant."

"Thank you," Levant said. He picked up the receiver. "Yes?"

Alfredo Pugnaci's gravelly voice was on the other end of the line. "Got a call from Ferril. That Apache police chief is back and has somebody else with him. They even offed some o' them Injuns last night."

"I see," Levant said. "I'm glad you called. Please make a trip out there and check the situation personally."

"Right."

Levant set the phone back in its cradle. Ferril was too much of an intellectual to properly judge the situation. Pugnaci, though barely able to read and write, was a pro who could properly assess and even advise on what to do.

Courtney looked at Levant. "You look a bit troubled."

Levant forced a smile. "Just a small business setback." Then his smile faded. "It will be taken care of very quickly."

8

Darkness is a man's best friend in time of danger.

Children's fear of the night could be easily dissipated if parents let them in on a secret: if you can't see the "bogeymen" lurking about in the inkiness, then they sure as hell can't see you, either.

It's that simple.

When fighting men have a vital need to seek out intelligence about the belligerent fellows opposing them, they prefer to do it at night. Proper movement in the darkness does not require the sort of spiritual magic attributed to the Oriental ninja, although the practitioners of this art are masters at nocturnal activities. However, no mysterious sorcery in the East makes the people there superior in deception and invisible movement. During the Second World War, the British SAS, the American Merrill's Marauders, Marine Raiders and Stillwell's Chindets used to run around the Japanese rear areas as if they owned the places.

All that is needed is the basic know-how, plenty of practice, and the balls to control fear when moving among folks who will happily blow your ass away if they discover your presence.

Reconnaissance during the hours of darkness under dangerous conditions was exactly what Dan Track and Steve Aguila were doing that particular night.

They became one with the blackness. Their hearing instinctively grew more acute; their feet moved through the manzanita with a stealth of their own, seeming to sense trouble such as dry twigs that would snap loudly. Track and Steve's night vision, enhanced with the quick, sideways darting of the eyes, brought dark shapes and movements to them in startling clarity.

Man is by nature a meat-eating hunter. Though not the strongest or fastest in the wild, he is the most intelligent, thus the deadliest. His stalking and scouting is not done by blind instinct; rather by skills, learned and honed through experience and intellect.

Part of this superior mental ability was evident in the way Track and Steve had prepared themselves. Their attire was perfect for the dangerous job they performed: tight fitting, to avoid snagging on brush; dark, to be less visible; and all external gear taped down to avoid any jangling or rustling.

Their faces were streaked with dark green and black camouflage paint, dulling the whiteness of Track's skin and eliminating the natural shininess of Steve's copper coloring. The weaponry they carried also reflected their need for silence. They carried only pistols and knives, secured to avoid slapping against their bodies during movment. The M-16s had been left back at the base camp in the Caballo Mountains.

The two barely breathed, yet drew in oxygen in efficient, short inhalations, as they glided slowly through the desert terrain.

Two silent, invisible killing machines.

They came down from the mountain and skirted the more populous area around the creek until they reached the point that Steve had identified as Geronimo Ferril's particular turf. Then they changed their trek and began the actual penetration of enemy territory.

Few dogs lived on the Llanero Reservation. Dogs require high-protein diets—impossible for a people struggling to feed themselves. And domestic animals were at the mercy of the wild animals—above all coyotes and cougars. The actual guarding of livestock was done by the owners themselves, or in most cases, by their young sons. This had been a boy's job in the Llanero tribe for as long as the people could remember. The sons had taken great pride in seeing that their fathers' horses were kept safe from enemy raiders.

Track and Steve, now having penetrated the major camping area, eased through the flocks, moving cautiously because of the boy guards. Both men knew that their man scent would not disturb the sheep or cattle. Most of the animals watched in sleepy curiosity, moving out of the way in slow irritation as the pair crawled among them in the darkness.

A small hill rose above the creek. Without vegetation of any sort, it would have offered no concealment during the day, but at night the little hill was a perfect place for an impromptu observation post. The irregular patterns of face paint and the tiger-striped fatigues made Track and Steve's concealment complete. Mother Nature is not a geometric designer. She works in shapes and colours that are mottled and varied. To hide within her realm it is necessary to avoid the straight, the symmetrical; in a natural setting order stands out like a streetwalker at a debutante ball. Even in the occasional patches of moonlight, Track and Steve did not attract the eye of any observers as they lay on the hill and peered down into the Apache encampment on the creek.

After several minutes, Steve put his mouth close to Track's ear and barely whispered. "The wickiup near the center, with the fire. That's Ferril's."

Track nodded and studied the structure. A fire illuminated the front of the dwelling. He could count two dozen men sitting in a crowded semicircle in front of the entrance. Their attention was focused on a powerful stocky figure in a red shirt who stood before them gesticulating. Track leaned close to Steve. "The red shirt—Ferril?"

Steve nodded.

Track studied this adversary for almost an hour. Now and then a wisp of breeze would carry a barely audible sample of Ferril's voice to them. It was deep and resonant. The man was a natural speaker and spellbinder.

At various times several men would stand up and leave the area to go to nearby wickiups—these were obviously lieutenants of some sort. Track surmised they had been given tasks and had withdrawn to discuss the execution of them. He noted their location in relation to Ferril's lodge.

By the time the meeting broke up, a little past midnight, Track had identified no less than six wickiups in the vicinity of Ferril's. On the next patrol, one to be designated as combat, he and Steve would have to move down into the village and do the job of a full squad of thirteen men. They would kill Ferril and his closest henchmen, then quickly withdraw to safety while a hundred or so pissed-off followers woke up and came charging after them.

It was a challenging project.

Track motioned for a withdrawal. They backed off the hill and into the draw behind it. Crouching, they started back when a juvenile voice suddenly called out. "Hey! Who's there?"

They both froze, slowly lowering themselves to the ground. Footsteps approached out of the darkness. The boy, silhouetted against the sky, was easy to see. Track wet his lips. He'd never killed a kid before. Not even in Vietnam where they skipped up playfully with grenades held in the loose sleeves of their shirts. Too weak to pull the pins, the adult Viet Cong did that for them. All the youngsters had to do was hold the safety spoon down, then release it before dropping the explosive device at the feet of unsuspecting Americans.

The situation caused Steve even more anguish. This was a child of his tribe, his people. As an Apache man, he was dedicated to protecting the young. His decision, if the situation forced it, must be made without hesitation. He had no choice. He would give himself up to save the boy and give Track the opportunity to haul ass.

The kid called out again. "Hey! Izzat you, Pablito? You better watch out!" He continued to approach the area where the two men lay motionless. Finally, without knowing it, he stood beside Track, peering around. He stepped forward and his small foot landed square on Track's hand.

Track grimaced, but held his breath. The kid probably weighed around a hundred pounds. The top of his hand wasn't designed to support that much weight.

"Pablito!" The kid, mercifully unaware he had been standing on a stranger's hand, walked up to the top of the hill where Track and Steve had been. He hollered out to his friend again. "You better answer me, wise guy!"

Track motioned back to Steve and the two melted away into the darkness, once again moving out into the safety of the desert.

9

The ghost dance began less than forty-eight hours after the television special for the Committee to Advance Native American Causes.

The ceremony commenced with a special ritual involving only the warriors. They retired to a place on the barren side of the Caballo Mountains. This area, protected from view by a natural wall of rocks and boulders, had been used for various religious and semimagical functions for as long as the Llanero Tribe could remember.

Here, sitting in their sweat lodges between bouts of fasting and chanting, the warriors gave themselves fully to the greater meaning of the ghost dance.

It began in the early morning chill and continued for a solemn thirty-six hours of non-stop meditation. When the time was right, Ferril led the warriors back down to the village where the women prepared an open area in the middle of the wickiups. Then the louder, more rambunctious part of the dance began with loud chanting, drums and dancing. Despite many hours of sleeplessness, the dancers were able to sustain their performance, renewing their energy with cold water and roasted venison.

Many of the celebrants went on for incredible periods of time before collapsing or being forcibly pulled out of the line of dancers to rest. The women were allowed to participate because, in the ancient tradition, their high-pitched voices were considered superior in attracting the spirits of the dead.

After another twenty-four hours, Geronimo set his plans into high gear. He was led to a position at the head of the drummers and signaled them to stop by raising and lowering his hand. Then he turned and faced his followers.

"The ghost dance has begun. We have fasted, gone into trances and danced as the customs of our tribe's medicine tell us to do. Now it is time to take the ghost dance further. All warriors know what they must do. I am now commanding them to take those actions for which they have made themselves ready."

With those words, Geronimo Ferril had issued the command to close off and isolate the Llanero Apache Reservation.

The first outsider to discover this extraordinary occurrence was Patrolman Tim Turnbull of the Arizona State Police when he arrived at the reservation to make the usual weekly delivery of wanted posters, reports and miscellaneous paperwork to the Apache police headquarters. A dozen weapon-packing residents blocked the normally empty and rather forlorn entrance into Llanero territory.

Turnbull eyed the armed men, all dressed in denims, boots and Stetson hats, milling around the area where the dirt road into the reservation joined the state highway. Not outwardly noisy, they appeared to be rather ordinary Arizona Indians. There were several pickup trucks parked nearby.

The group, however, did have an air of impatience about it. The policeman's instincts told him that there was something dangerous about it all, but his logical side took over and he continued to approach them. Finally, he brought his unit to a gradual stop and leaned his head out the window. "You guys going hunting?" he asked. All appearances suggested that that was what they were preparing to do.

A burly Apache, looking decidedly unfriendly, a Ruger model 77 rifle over one shoulder, walked up to the police vehicle. He ignored Turnbull's question. "What's your business here?"

"I'm on my way to the reservation police." Turnbull glanced at the other members of the small crowd looking his way. His original uneasiness began to grow.

The Indian laughed. "You mean you *were* on your way. The Llanero Apache Nation is sealed off from outsiders."

Turnbull, angry enough now to forget his nervousness, spoke in a loud voice. "What the hell do you mean *nation*?"

"We've made our own Declaration of Independence," the Indian answered.

"By who's goddamned authority?" Turnbull demanded.

The rifle came off the shoulder and ended up with the bore leveled straight at the policeman's head. "Me, Geronimo Ferril, and ol' Betsy here. This committee of three tells you to haul ass."

And that's what Turnbull did.

TREVOR LEVANT SAT on his patio enjoying both the sea view and a leisurely breakfast of French toast and sausage. He ate alone, preferring not to have an attending servant at his favorite meal of the day. Levant savored each mouthful of the well-prepared meal, consuming the food off the expensive china breakfast dishes. He had purchased the elegant tableware during a tour of Beverly Hills shops a scant two weeks previously.

Levant had just poured himself a cup of coffee from the silver urn by his elbow when his houseboy appeared with a telephone. Wordlessly, the servant plugged it in and set the instrument down beside his employer.

Levant picked up the receiver. "Yeah?"

"This is Pugnaci," said the gravelly voice on the other end. "They done it like they was supposed to."

"Is the reservation sealed off?"

"Tighter'n a nun's pussy."

"Thank you, Pugnaci," Levant said. "Both the news you just gave me and the analogy you used to describe its effectiveness have started this day out wonderfully for me."

"Right."

Levant pushed the disconnect button, then quickly punched out a Hollywood number. He waited until the call was answered by a crisply efficient female voice saying, "Mister Courtney's office."

"Hello, Donna. This is Trevor Levant. May I speak to Jerry?"

"Oh, hello, Mister Levant! Mister Courtney is on location. Shall I have him paged?"

"Please do, Donna. This is terribly important."

"Of course."

"He'll be able to reach me at home anytime this morning."

Levant hung up. Smiling in happy anticipation, he turned his attention back to the coffee while he savored in his mind the news he had just received.

THE HONORABLE Bruce Babbitt, Governor of the State of Arizona, had called a meeting of his cabinet. Several important items were originally scheduled for discussion with his top-ranking subordinates. Both policy and decisions had to be firmed up regularly in order to keep a smooth-running administration functioning along the lines the voters demanded.

The secretary of state, Rose Mofford, had shown up on time, but after nearly twenty minutes of waiting, both she and Babbitt were irritated. The state's attorney general seemed to be running late that morning. When Arizona's top lawyer made his appearance, his boss was mildly caustic. "I hope it was something important involving the public that's the cause of your tardiness, Bob."

Bob Corbin nodded a curt greeting to the other two. He dropped his briefcase on the large conference table. The expression on his face gave every indication that something was indeed awry in the state of Arizona. "I received a call about two hours ago, Governor. The Indians on the Llanero Apache Reservation have sealed it off and won't let any outsiders in."

"Did you have this confirmed?" the governor asked.

"Yes. I dispatched Reilly and Billsby from my staff. I've just gotten off the phone with them. There are picket lines—although 'skirmish' lines might be more accurate—blocking off all normal entrances to the reservation."

"Have there been any demands made or reasons given?"

"Not so far," Corbin answered. "There's no display of signs or posters with slogans or announcements. And since no spokespersons have stepped forward, we don't know who's in charge of the affair."

Babbitt thought quickly. "Okay. First thing—no interference. This is a federal matter, but it's happening within the state. I do not—repeat—do not want any overreaction from any Arizona law personnel."

"Right," Corbin said. "We received a report on the situation from a state trooper who was blocked from making a routine administrative call on the Apache police. He quickly withdrew under threat. So far, I've put extra men on alert, and I'll be holding them a few miles away at Pearce."

Secretary Mofford was concerned. "We shouldn't have to call out the National Guard to back them up unless the trouble spills out of U.S. Government lands and jurisdiction."

"Right. Let's alert the adjutant general and order him to follow SOP for a possible emergency," the governor ordered in crisp tones. "But keep everything low keyed."

"I'm on my way," the secretary of state said.

"Has the news media made an appearance?" Babbitt asked.

"Not yet. But an announcement will have to be made shortly if the situation continues," Corbin said. "I hope we're not about to get a real live Indian war breaking out."

"Well," the governor mused, "that would be a rather redundant addition to what is already recorded in the history books of this state."

"I pray things don't go that far," Corbin said grimly.

JEROME COURTNEY REFERRED to the script in his hand several times as he watched the scene being shot. The two actors, playing the roles of gangster and detective in Courtney's highly rated crime series, began the confrontation that was story-boarded to end up in a bloody fistfight. They played it right up to the action bit, then the director ordered an end to things with a curt, "Cut!"

At that point, two skilled and experienced stuntmen stepped in to prepare for the long shots of the fight. Their expertise and daring would make it realistic enough for a blood-thirsty public.

Courtney took advantage of the lull in the proceedings to walk over to his limousine and answer his pager's beeper on the car telephone. A few quick words with Donna, his secretary, informed him that Trevor Levant had tried to reach him. Courtney wasted no time in returning the call.

"Trevor, this is Jerry. Donna said you called."

"Thank God!" Levant replied. "I was afraid you would be unreachable. Do you remember my friend Geronimo Ferril?"

"Yes, yes of course," Courtney replied. "Is there something wrong, Trevor?"

"In a way there is, yet taking all under consideration it's a rather glorious thing."

"What in the world is going on?"

"Geronimo and his people have completely taken over the Llanero reservation and sealed it off from outsiders," Levant said. "I've only just now received a call from someone I know on the scene. The Llanero people are proclaiming themselves an independent nation!"

"My God! What prompted that?"

Trevor Levant paused for affect. "Need you ask?"

"I shouldn't have had to, really," Courtney admitted. "It sounds much like the proverbial straw that broke the camel's back. One injustice too many has led to a reaction."

"Finally! After all these years, and I'm most pleased about it," Levant said. "They'll do more in the next few weeks than we could accomplish in years in CANAC."

"You're right, of course," Courtney said. He sighed. "We Hollywood types are really such wimps when it comes to real revolution. We sit around wearing our Gucci and Lauren and—" he stopped speaking for a few seconds "—Listen to me jabbering when there're things to be done. Do you have any suggestions, Trevor?"

"Yes! Yes, of course," Levant said. "Our Apache friends are facing great danger. My contact on the reservation tells me that both local and federal lawmen are closing in on them, and closing in fast!" He took a breath to let the falsehood sink in. "We must get them help. I was thinking of your friend Senator O'Connor. He's very sympathetic to CANAC, is he not?"

"He's an avid and outspoken supporter," Courtney said. "I'm certain he would be most happy to lend his influence to this situation."

"Is he in town?"

"He's in Washington," Courtney replied.

"Then you must contact him now—*now!* Have him call off those dogs. Then you and I must get out to Arizona as quickly as possible. Geronimo said he would like to talk to us—both of us."

"I'm honored—really!" Courtney said. "And of course I'll try to get hold of Ted immediately. It may take a while."

"Please, hurry. I'll see to arranging transportation."

"Let me give you the number of a charter air service I use quite frequently. I usually keep a plane on call there during the series shoots. I know the owner quite well. I'll insist he fly us personally."

"Great, Jerry. My God, man! Let's get moving on this before our Llanero friends are massacred by the army or police!"

"Yes, of course," Jerome Courtney said fumbling with his wallet to get the air company's business card.

On the other end of the line Trevor Levant grinned. His scheme was rolling into its opening phases.

GERONIMO FERRIL was angry.

Now, after five hours, his blockade and isolation of the reservation had not resulted in one confrontation with the authorities.

He sat in the cab of the pickup looking out over the intersection where the state highway and the reservation's main road came together. Aside from his own people walking listlessly back and forth, there was nothing.

Beside him, his number one war chief, Roberto Lobo, idly drummed the steering wheel. "It don't look like too many folks give a shit about this."

"Things will change," Ferril promised. They continued to sit for another quarter of an hour, then suddenly the Apache leader brightened. "I know where there'll be problems."

The realization dawned on Lobo too. "Right. The southwest entrance—the fucking Border Patrol."

"The way things have been going between the United States and Mexico, those 'boys in green' ought to be real nervous," Ferril said.

"The trick is to force them to make the first moves," Lobo reminded him.

Ferril smiled. "So... let's get tricky."

Lobo hit the starter, then turned the vehicle around, its wheels spinning on the sandy roadbed.

THE RADIO in the Willys jeep wagon crackled. "Unit Five, how's the situation out there?"

The border patrolman, comfortably situated on the front seat, lazily answered. "This is Unit Five. Same old stuff. I'm here on my butt across the road."

"Any unusual activity?" asked the other voice.

The lawman glanced at the ten Apaches, heavily armed with everything from hunting rifles to assault weapons, warily watching him. This peaceful confrontation had been going on since early morning. The patrolman, ordered to stand fast, had been doing that for four hours.

He hit the mike button. "No developments, like I said. They're looking at me. I'm looking at them."

"Continue the drill."

"Ten-four."

Since the lessening of illegal-alien activity along the southern part of the Apache reservation, the Border Patrol had thinned out their surveillance of the area. They knew something unusual was going on. Snitches among the coyotes had given them information that groups of Mexicans were sneaking into one side of Llanero country, but not coming out the other. Even a couple of professional people-smugglers were among the missing. It was a mystery as to the exact cause of the situation. Most of the agents chalked it up to a war among the coyotes similar to feuds among the minor narcotics czars. It would blow over soon. When it did, there would be another influx of illegals trying to get to the rich land of the *norteamericanos* and the jobs available there.

In the meantime, the local supervisor took advantage of the slow period to transfer men to busier spots closer to Nogales.

"Unit Four."

"Ten-four."

"C'mon in. Leave the area as quickly as possible and report back to headquarters," the radio voice ordered.

"Ten-four. Whose orders? The superintendent's?"

The dispatcher hadn't had much to talk about lately. He felt chatty. "Roger. By way of Senator O'Connor of California."

The patrolman took another look at the surly Indians. "Shit," he said to himself, "with O'Connor sticking his nose into all this, there'll be a thousand demonstrators here by early evening."

He gunned the motor, and drove out on the road turning west toward McNeal.

At almost the precise moment he left the scene, Ferril and Lobo drove up to the pickets. Ferril stepped out of the truck before it came to a complete halt.

He glanced outward toward the open desert as he approached the other Apaches. "Didn't the Border Patrol try to come in for their regular scouting work?"

Rick Pantera, the war chief assigned to the south, shrugged. "Ever since this morning the guy was just sitting on the other side of the road watching us. Then he suddenly left just as you drove up."

Ferril spat. Getting some violence into this situation is going to take some doing, he thought, but Trevor Levant is just the boy to make it happen.

10

Track lowered the binoculars from his eyes. He turned his head and glanced under his arm at Steve Aguila who stood below and slightly behind the observation position. This natural groove in the rocks was overgrown with vegetation, leaving barely enough room for a man to wiggle in and peer out from the craggy mountains down to the open desert below.

Track glanced at his Rolex Sea Dweller watch. He was surprised to note that he'd just spent three solid hours observing the barren countryside. He felt agitated and uneasy with the nervous energy of a hungry tiger. Something was definitely out of the ordinary for even an unusually hairy situation like the one he and Steve were in at the moment. And until Track could figure out exactly what was going on, his whole being would be consumed by uneasiness.

Now, eyes burning with fatigue, he pushed himself out of the crag and slid down to join his friend.

"What the hell do you make of things?" Steve asked.

"There's some rare shit going down all right," Track said shoving the binoculars back into their case. "Today has been a hell of a lot different than whatever's been going on since we got here. From the looks of things, I'd say they've lost some of their interest in us. The number of patrols seems to be down by at least half."

"Maybe they're exchanging quantity for quality," Steve mused. "Fewer patrols, fewer activities . . . then, out of the blue, they held that dance." He instinctively looked out toward the desert even though the wall of rock blocked his view. "Now everything is damned near like a tomb out there."

"Puzzling," Track remarked remembering how well the night sounds of the Indian ceremony had carried across the space of sand and rocks. The staccato rhythms combined with the baritone voices of men and the shrill of feminine voices had blended into a peculiar and diabolical symphony. Track estimated the goings-on were nearly ten miles away, yet the chanting and the pounding drums had been clear and resonant. He looked at Steve. "Are you sure there's no special Apache holiday or other reason for celebration? It would have to be damned important to divert most of their attention from us."

Steve slowly shook his head. "I can't think of a damn thing, Dan. There's no Llanero religious or normal ceremonial stuff due at this time of year that I can think of. Maybe Ferril is just letting them blow off steam."

"I really doubt that," Track said. "If that was his motive, he'd send all of 'em up here looking for us. A good way for them to relieve the tension would be to blow us away—or at least burn up nervous energy looking for us. And as far as I can tell, there hasn't been much movement our way for the past day or so. Maybe that ghost dance you've been talking about is finally taking place."

"That's one bit of Indian custom that I'm not all that familiar with. I know the meaning of it, but the actual protocol is a mystery to me. Ferril knows it from an intense study of the tribe," Steve said. "At any rate, there's only one way we're going to find out what's going on," Steve said. "We've got to go back down there."

"You're right," Track said. "Putting it off won't make things a damned bit easier. Let's get our gear rigged for silent movement and head back out into the cold after dark."

"Okay. What is it this time? Reconnaissance or combat?"

"We'll play it by ear," Track said. "But I would like to get my hands on a car or pickup. How's your hot-wiring technique?"

"That won't be necessary," Steve said. "Everybody leaves their keys in their vehicles."

"That's handy," Track said.

"It sure is," Steve agreed. "The only time we have to lock our cars is when we go into town." Then he added with a grin. "You know how it is around civilized folks."

"I know what you mean."

"What do you want with a vehicle?"

"The same thing Rommel would want," Track said. "To go for a little fast maneuvering across the desert."

THE LEAR JET BANKED gracefully, then dropped rapidly through the thin air toward the short runway of Sierra Vista's airport. The airfield was not designed to serve any large airliners, and even bringing the smaller Lear in took all the skills of the pilot.

Trevor Levant and Jerome Courtney sat inside the passenger's compartment on opposite sides of the aisle. Each peered out at the heat waves dancing across the concrete. They both grimaced as the wheels touched down and the brakes were applied in conjunction with the reversed engines, which roared their protest against the plane's forward momentum. Levant gripped the armrests so hard that his hands ached with the effort. He didn't relax his hold until the aircraft finally came to a stop close to the airport's small operations building.

The whine of the engines died gradually and an eerie silence took its place.

The pilot, a stocky, red-haired ex-marine pilot with a neatly trimmed mustache, stepped out of the cockpit. He nodded to Courtney. "Sierra Vista, Arizona. As requested."

"Thank you, Sherman," Jerome Courtney said. "A very nice flight."

"Glad you enjoyed it," Sherman said. "Do you still want me to wait?"

"If you can manage," Courtney said finally undoing his seat belt. "I'm certain we can use you for the next two or three days. Perhaps even a week."

"I can manage that," Sherman said. "But I'll have to check in with my office."

Trevor Levant got to his feet and stepped unsteadily into the aisle. "We may need you for several more trips between here and L.A. and back."

"No problem," Sherman said. "I'll see to gassing up right away." He opened the door in the side of the fuselage and pushed it upward. A slight kick of his foot forced a set of steps outward and down to the runway. Sherman stepped down first and stood aside as Levant and Courtney disembarked.

"We'll be in touch," Courtney said to the pilot.

"I'll stand by," Sherman promised.

Levant, who was deathly afraid of flying, felt a sense of great relief as his feet hit the reassuring solidity of the runway. He glanced around expectantly, then waved at a heavyset man approaching them. "There's my friend."

Courtney watched as the stranger approached. "Mmmm. Doesn't look like an Indian to me."

Levant smiled. "Perhaps he's more like a Hollywood Indian, Jerry. He's actually Italian."

Pugnaci walked up and extended his hand. "Hi ya, Mr. Levant. I see you're here."

"How perceptive of you," Levant said. He pointed toward his companion. "This is Mr. Courtney."

"Hi ya," Pugnaci said. "The handle is Al, Al Pugnaci."

"How are you?" Courtney inquired. "I understand you've been with the demonstration from the start."

"Even before," Pugnaci said. He looked at Levant. "I got the car on the other side o' this building." He swung his eyes back to Courtney. "The shit's gonna hit the fan pretty damn quick."

Courtney felt uneasy around the big man. The heavy, half-closed eyes had a threatening quality about them. The gruff voice booming out of that heavy, dark body did little to put him at ease either. If Courtney were to cast this man in any of his television shows, it most certainly would be as a sadistic heavy. He felt nervous, but he put on a friendly front. "Lot of trouble, hey?"

"Yeah," Pugnaci said. He took a deep breath and recited, "The Llanero Injuns is being brutalized and harassed to such a extent, their lives are in danger." He made a motion with his head. "C'mon. I'll take youse to the car."

Courtney's outrage overshadowed his jitters. "What's happening, Mr. Pugnaci? Have the authorities attacked the Indians? Have there been serious injuries? Anyone killed?"

"It's better if you take a look for yourself," Pugnaci said leading the way.

The three men walked around the building to an air-conditioned Mercedes. Pugnaci opened the back door for Levant and Courtney, then went around to the driver's side.

Courtney, puzzled, leaned forward as Pugnaci settled himself behind the wheel. "Uh . . . what sort of business are you in, Mr. Pugnaci?"

"I work for Mr. Levant."

"Really?" Courtney looked at Levant. "Do you have a real-estate business interest out here? I thought all your dealings were in southern California."

Levant smiled easily. "Mr. Pugnaci is a member of my administrative staff. I had planned to set up an Arizona office, so I transferred him east some time ago. In the meantime I heard from my old friend Geronimo Ferril, so I delayed organizing the business and asked Mr. Pugnaci to keep an eye on things. Later I learned just how serious the situation had become, so I'm glad I took these precautionary steps."

"The delay in establishing your business must have been very costly, Trevor," Courtney exclaimed. "How very generous of you!"

"One does what one must," Levant said in a modest tone.

The two settled into quiet but earnest conversation as Pugnaci drove out of the hilly country, north to the flatter area of desert where Llanero country was located. He broke his silence after an hour, pointing to the purplish mountains that now rose from the sandy horizon. "Them's the Caballo mountains," Pugnaci said. Then he added, "that means 'horse' in Spanish. That's real close to *cavallo*—that's the way it's said in Italian."

"Interesting," Levant remarked insincerely. "How far to our destination?"

"Another thirty or forty-five minutes," Pugnaci said.

"Make that thirty minutes," Levant said in a firm voice.

"Right."

The expensive car sped up under the big man's control, its slipstream whipping up grainy dust alongside the road.

GERONIMO FERRIL checked his watch. It was early afternoon with the sun sinking in its slow but relentless path toward the mountainous horizon to the west. He took another look across the road. There were three patrol cars from the Arizona State Police. They had arrived there an hour after the one cop had been sent packing. Since that time hardly a word had been exchanged between the officers and the Indians who still stood defiantly at the entrance to their reservation.

Roberto Lobo, his Smith and Wesson .38 riding low in the holster on his hip, sauntered casually out onto the macadam of the main road and glanced up and down. He took a steady, cold look at the police, then turned and slowly walked back to Geronimo Ferril.

Lobo shrugged. "Still no sign of the Feds."

"Damn!" Ferril said under his breath. "I'd hoped to be in the middle of a noisy confrontation by now."

"What pisses me off about the thing is that we ain't been giving the proper attention to Steve Aguila and whoever it is with him."

"Those two don't pose a serious threat now. A few patrols should keep that pair off balance," Ferril said. "Once we get both the ghost dance and the fight with the law going, anybody on the reservation who hasn't joined us will be in the right frame of mind to help us kick ass."

Lobo looked back at the state police. "Them guys ain't doing shit."

Ferril remembered Levant's instructions that if no real confrontations occurred quickly, he must create some. He motioned to Lobo. "Then we'll liven up their day."

"Time to start, huh?" Lobo asked.

"Time to start," Ferril confirmed.

"Want me to warn the other guys?" Lobo asked.

"We need some martyrs," Ferril said coolly.

Lobo nodded. He walked over to his pickup and pulled a Ruger mini-14 from the cab. Once more strolling easily, this time with the carbine held behind him out of sight of the policemen, he walked back up to the road. Again he paused, looking slowly up and down the country road. Then he looked at the cops.

"Hey! Assholes!"

He brought up the weapon and pumped off the magazine, spraying rounds into the police vehicles. Glass shattered and bullets whined as they skidded off the autos, or smacked loudly as they punched into them. One of the policemen, his body jerking with each impact of the bullets that struck him, backpedaled a couple of yards until he collided with the rear fender of his car. Then his head exploded under the wallop of a higher round, sending a redish-gray spray of brains over the top of the automobile.

The other two lawmen had cleared leather quickly. They fired rapidly, skillfully covering each other as they retreated to a gully behind the point where they'd stationed themselves.

One of the Indians, as surprised by Lobo's action as the cops, had stood transfixed. He took a .38 round in the pelvis that careered up into the intestines. He went immediately into shock, slowly turning to stagger back before pitching face down into the dirt.

At the same time, another Apache was whipped to the ground when one leg buckled backward under the blow of a .44 Magnum round. The cop with the bigger gun was faster and more accurate than his partner. He fired twice more, one bullet tearing away a fat hunk of deltoid muscle, rolling the Indian over to expose his chest. The next bullet hit there, shoving the victim into a quarter spin. The man was dead before the dust had settled.

The surviving police finally dived into the ravine. They didn't waste time congratulating themselves for escaping. The pair continued to throw out a protective hail of lead toward the Apaches.

America's twentieth-century Indian war was on.

11

Pugnaci applied the brakes, pointing straight ahead with one beefy hand while holding on to the steering wheel with the other. "Looks like a problem in the road."

Trevor Levant and Jerome Courtney both leaned forward to peer over the front seat through the windshield of the Mercedes. They could see a barricade set across the highway. There were several police cars parked off on the shoulders with one situated sideways behind the blocked area in case someone decided to break through the barrier. The lawmen standing there wore riot gear and carried shotguns.

Pugnaci slowed to a crawl then stopped directly in front of an officer who signaled the halt. The officer, stooping slightly to observe the inside of the expensive automobile, approached cautiously.

Pugnaci lowered the window letting the hot outside air invade the air-conditioned interior. "What's up, officer?"

"The road is closed," the policeman said. "May I ask where you're going?"

Jerome Courtney glared at the lawman. He could feel old resentments from the Days-of-Rage protests during the Vietnam War surfacing. "Why is the highway blocked?" he demanded.

The policeman ignored the question. "What's your destination please?"

Courtney noted the man's name tag identified him as Officer T. Turnbull. "Our trip is our business," Courtney said hotly. "And so is the reason for our being unable to continue. Therefore, I repeat—why is the highway barricaded?"

"Routine," Turnbull said.

"Routine, hell!" Courtney hissed. "Now, goddamn it! You answer my question!"

Trevor Levant, with a few habits left over from his days in the Massachusetts state prison system, played the con's dumb game waiting to see what developed. Pugnaci, a man not known to waste time, took the opportunity to switch on the radio and dial for an all-news station out of Tucson he was familiar with. He kept the volume down as he listened to it with one ear, keeping the other tuned in on the argument that was developing between Courtney and the policeman.

"You cannot arbitrarily block a public thoroughfare without rhyme or reason," Courtney said. "I demand to know the reason and I demand to know it now—*now!*"

"Routine," Turnbull said doggedly. But this time he added, "By the order of the state attorney general."

They continued the useless conversation for another five minutes until Pugnaci's attention was grabbed by the radio. Without hesitating, he kicked the volume up high. The amplified voice of the newscaster blared out:

"The stand-off between the state police and the demonstrating inhabitants of the Llanero Apache Reservation continues. While no official announcements have been made, it has been established that there have been casualties—both policemen and Indians—in a shoot-out that occurred a few hours ago. Details are sketchy, but it is known that several Apaches have been shot. Police—"

"*You fucking pigs*!"

Jerome Courtney, generally low-keyed and under control, had come unglued. He pushed against the car door, forcing it open, then charged outside.

"Grab him, Pugnaci!" Levant ordered.

In spite of his bulk, Al Pugnaci moved fast and efficiently. He intercepted the enraged TV producer, holding the struggling man in a tight bear hug from the back as he tried to get at the policeman.

Tim Turnbull stared coldly at the screaming man. "The incident was provoked by the Indians," he said.

"That's a goddamned rotten lie!" Courtney yelled. "Those poor people were gunned down in cold blood by you bastards!"

"Please get back into the car, Jerry," Levant said from the open door. "There's nothing we can do here now."

"Hell, no! I'm going to kill these sons of bitches!" Courtney yelled.

Levant motioned with a nod of his head. Taking his cue, Pugnaci lifted Courtney off the ground and carried him back to the automobile. Courtney had calmed down slightly by the time Pugnaci gently pushed him into the back seat.

"I'm all right," he said.

"You sure?" Pugnaci asked.

Courtney took a deep breath. "Yes."

"Let him go," Levant said.

Courtney glared out at the barricade. "The bastards! The dirty bastards!" He fought down his anger as it started to grow again. "We've got to be cool, Trevor."

"Of course."

"Wasn't there a diner a few miles back?"

"Yeah," Pugnaci answered.

"Let's get back there," Courtney said getting into the car. "I've got some calls to make."

"We're on our way," Levant said.

Pugnaci jumped back into the driver's seat. After starting the engine, he turned from the shoulder onto the highway and drove back in the direction from which they'd come.

A scant five minutes later the Mercedes pulled up in front of a nondescript, cheap highway eatery identifying itself by a hand-lettered sign as Lingenfelder's Diner. It also boasted home-cooked meals and air-conditioned comfort. The owner of the place, Orv Lingenfelder, sat comfortably behind the counter reading a copy of the *Tucson Daily Star*. He looked up in happy anticipation at the entrance of the three men. His expression faded somewhat when they went directly to the pay phone by a broken, dusty pin-ball machine.

"May we have change for the phone?" Courtney asked.

"Hell, no! I ain't got enough for that," Lingenfelder said. Then he added hopefully, "You gents want something to eat?"

"Did we order something?" Pugnaci asked glowering.

"Naw, you didn't order nothing."

"Then we don't want nothing."

"I still ain't got change for the goddamned phone," the diner owner insisted.

"Never mind, I can use my credit card," Courtney said. He picked up the phone and dialed the numbers for a call to Washington, D.C. As he waited for the connection to go through, he turned to Levant. "I'm getting hold of Ted O'Connor—*Senator* Ted O'Connor. He was going to hold a special investigation of this incident. But now we'll get some action and so goddamned quick those pigs won't know what happened to them."

Levant, thinking fast, spoke up. "Tell him the Indians need food, Jerry. And medicine. I'll arrange for the trucks if he can get safe passage for them in and out of the reservation."

Courtney's eyes lit up. "Right! Good thinking, Trevor. I would never have—" he quickly turned his attention back to the call as the operator came on the line "—I want to speak directly and quickly with Senator Ted O'Connor. My name is Jerome Courtney, and this is of the utmost urgency."

Pugnaci grinned, then walked over to the counter. Levant's trucks might go in there full of food and medicine, but they'd be coming out with something better than gold. He glanced at the cook. "Hey! Gimme a cup o' coffee."

"Get us some too, Pugnaci," Levant said.

"Right."

"Make mine iced tea, please," Courtney said.

Pugnaci grinned again. The narcotics scam was about to go into full swing. In fact, he estimated the stuff ought to be on the way to city streets within twenty-four hours.

12

Dan Track and Steve Aguila bent almost double as they moved rapidly and quietly down the ravine. Above the six-foot bank, they could see light dancing from the fire that had attracted them to that particular spot.

After traveling fifty yards, they stopped and squatted in the protective shadows of this cut in the desert floor. Steve leaned close to his friend and whispered, "Well? What the hell do you make of that?"

They had just spent five minutes observing a group of Llanero Apaches gathered in what appeared to be a fighting formation across an entrance road to the reservation.

Track had found it relatively easy to figure out what was happening. "Obviously they're blocking the way into Llanero land. That part's easy. The tough thing to figure out is why."

"That bastard Ferril has some real weird shit going down, man," Steve said angrily. "And now it's a hundred-and-eighty-degree turnaround from what he was doing before. At first he was keeping a tight lid on things and maintaining a real low profile. Blocking off the reservation will call plenty of attention to him now."

"That gunfire we heard late yesterday can probably be tied in to this thing," Track said. "We've got to take a look at the other entrances to the reservation. I'd bet my SPAS-12 we're witnessing the beginning of outright warfare." His mind turned over what he'd seen on the maps he had studied. "There must be at least a half dozen roads into the place."

"Yeah," Steve said. "And scattered around a hundred or so square miles. It'd take forever to recon 'em on foot." Then he added in an excited tone, "You have a SPAS-12?"

"You bet," Track answered. "One of the smartest purchases I've ever made."

"Jesus! Is that thing as good as they say?"

"Better," Track said. "But we're digressing."

"I suppose we are," Steve said. "So what's our next move?"

"We steal a vehicle," Track said.

"The nearest ones are with our friends back at that fire," Steve said.

"Too much activity there. What about one of the camps by the creek?"

"I'd say that's the best bet," Steve said.

"Okay. We'll go over that way and find a quiet one. Or at least someplace where the opportunity to rip off some wheels is better than here."

The two spent a few more minutes listening for activity around or near them. Then they resumed the short journey down to the end of the ravine and turned out into the open desert that lay between them and the scattered bivouacs of reservation dwellers.

OFFICER TIM TURNBULL was so mad he could have bitten through the barrel of a .357. Not only was one good cop down, but it happened to be one of his best friends. Turnbull knew he'd be tagged with informing the widow.

Now, with his buddy's body still lying between a trio of shot-out patrol cars and the main entrance onto the Llanero Apache Reservation, orders had come down to allow a semitrailer full of food and medicine to pass through police lines and go to the Indians.

It was close to 10:00 P.M. when the eight-wheeler arrived complete with an escort of two motorcycles and a lieutenant and his driver in a patrol unit. Turnbull brought the small convoy to a halt by holding an upraised hand. When the lieutenant's car pulled up beside him, he stuck his head inside. "What's up, Lieutenant?"

"Goodies for the folks on the reservation," the lieutenant replied.

"Whose big idea was this anyway?" Turnbull exclaimed.

The lieutenant shook his head. "The goody two-shoes have stuck their noses into this affair."

"Yeah? Well, I'm going to search that truck, Lieutenant."

"It's already been checked out," the lieutenant said. "There's canned goods and some first-aid supplies in the trailer."

Turnbull was adamant. "It ain't coming through here without my clearance, Lieutenant."

"Now see here—"

"No! *You* see here," Turnbull said. "I'm in charge of this roadblock. That's the same as a sentry in the military service having responsibility for his post. It don't come through here unless I say it does."

The lieutenant was angry. "Goddamn it, Turnbull! This situation is touchy enough without you adding to it."

"Either get me written orders relieving me of duty here or tell that fucking trucker to open up the back of the trailer," Turnbull said.

At that point, the truck driver stepped down from the cab and approached the two officers. "What's the holdup here?"

"We're checking out your cargo, pal," Turnbull said.

"Bullshit!" the trucker snarled. "You cops already—"

Turnbull grabbed the man and shoved him hard against the lieutenant's car. "Give me any shit, asshole, and I'll spread your fucking nose all over your face!"

"Okay! Okay!" the trucker said. He twisted out of Turnbull's grasp and walked back toward the back of the trailer. "Jesus Christ! Let somebody shoot some of you cops and you take it out on the whole world!"

STEVE AGUILA POINTED to the small bivouac fifty yards away. "That'll be where the Culebra brothers live," he said to Track.

"Anything special about them?"

"They're two of the meanest sons of bitches I've ever met," Steve said. "They've spent plenty of time inside the reservation jailhouse. I had to send a couple of my men out a few times every month to arrest 'em for drunkenness and brawling."

"Hardcases, huh?" Track asked.

"I'll say! They're two of the worst examples of reservation Indians I've ever seen. They're constantly bickering and fighting with their neighbors, and can barely tolerate each other. But let me warn you—don't get 'em both mad at you at the same time."

Track snorted. "Hell! I don't want to piss 'em off. I just want to steal one of their trucks."

"They're antisocial, Dan," Steve said.

"Is that why they're camped way out here by themselves?" Track asked.

Steve nodded. "Right. I don't think even Geronimo Ferril wanted anything to do with them."

"Like I said, the only thing I'm interested in is their vehicles," Track said. "I really don't like to borrow a guy's wheels without asking, but from the way you described them, I don't think they'd cooperate much."

"Their motto is Always Say 'No' Unless There's a Good Reason to Say 'No Fucking Way.'" I think it would be smarter to sneak in there and just drive off."

"I agree," Track said.

Their destination was a miserable-looking encampment made up of two tents so weatherbeaten and faded that even in the moonlight their poor condition was easily visible. Unlike the other areas used by the Llaneros, this one was messy. Trash, two stripped autos, a stack of old tires and other debris littered the space around the tents. A hurricane lamp hissed inside one of the domiciles, its light showing through the holes in the canvas.

Steve laughed a little and sang softly, "Be it ever so humble, there's no place like home."

They walked carefully, making sure they didn't accidentally kick a discarded beer can or send some empty whiskey bottle rolling into something. There were two pickup trucks parked on opposite sides of the camp. Track nudged Steve. "Which of those junk heaps do you think runs the best?"

"Don't let the outside appearance fool you," Steve said. "Both the Culebras are good mechanics. They don't give a damn what their vehicles look like, but I can guarantee you that those engines are in top-notch condition. As a matter of fact, they earn their drinking money with part-time work in various town garages ."

Track pointed to the nearest truck. "Well, let's check out that baby."

They walked up the small rise to where the vehicle was parked.

"You want to drive, as usual?" Steve asked.

"I'd better not. You know this area better than I do," Track answered. "And there may be some quick decisions that have to be made without the benefit of prolonged counsel."

"Gee! I love that kind of fancy talk. I almost re-upped in the army on account of bullshit like that," Steve said. He had gone around to the driver's side as Track reached out for the handle on the passenger's door.

"Hold it!"

Track spun and found himself looking at a shirtless Indian rising to a standing position from behind a small manzanita bush. He was about as friendly-looking as the bore of the Stevens-Savage 12-gauge shotgun he had leveled dead on Track's belly.

And from the voices on the other side of the truck, Track knew that Steve also had a welcoming party.

OFFICER TURNBULL had his heels locked.

The captain had shown up at the roadblock with his temper boiling. He didn't give a damn about Turnbull's personal feelings about his dead friend, or about the fact the policeman had been on the job there for close to thirty hours. But he was concerned about the fact Turnbull had delayed the food shipment into the reservation by searching the truck.

"You're lucky there were no newsmen here at the time!" the captain shouted.

"Yes, sir," Turnbull replied dully.

"It was bad enough that goddamned driver called his boss back in California and told him what you'd done," the captain railed on. "The son of a bitch is a friend of Jerome Courtney, the big TV bastard who's made this whole situation a personal crusade of his!"

Turnbull rubbed a hand across his face. "Yes, sir."

"There's gonna be a shitpot full of newspeople here by daybreak, Turnbull," the captain said. "And they will be here to record the trucks of supplies going into that fucking reservation. Do you understand that?"

"Right, Cap'n."

"And some of the pictures they'll be showing the viewing public will be the benevolent officers of the Arizona State Police allowing the vehicles through on their mission of mercy."

"What if there's ammo or arms in those trucks, Cap'n?" Turnbull asked.

"Jesus Christ! You think Jerome Courtney is going to foment a war? He was a peace demonstrator during the Vietnam War. The bastard is a pacifist."

"Oh, yeah? He's done plenty of war stuff on television and in the movies," Turnbull countered.

"How the man makes his money and what his personal philosophy is are two separate things," the captain said.

"Yeah, but—"

"Don't search those trucks when they go into the reservation and don't search them when they come out. Got it, Turnbull?"

Turnbull sighed. "Yes, Cap'n."

TRACK AND STEVE stood in front of the truck with their hands raised high. The Culebra brothers—Eduardo and Ricardo—had the drop on them. Eduardo was the one with the shotgun. Ricardo held a Winchester Model 94. Although worn, both weapons appeared to be in extremely good operable condition—particularly from where Track and Steve stood.

Eduardo, a little drunk, looked quizzically at Steve. "Where'n hell you been? I ain't seen you for a while."

His brother Ricardo had a better memory. "Don't you remember, you dumb shit? Him and Geronimo Ferril tangled assholes." He laughed. "All his little boys in blue got blowed away."

Eduardo's attitude turned even more sour. "Yeah! Tha's right. You went against Ferril, didn't you? You want us all to be good li'l Injun boys so the Fed'rals can keep screwing us over, right?"

"Listen to me," Steve said angrily. "That—"

"Don't you tell me nothing!" Eduardo shouted. "You ain't throwing my ass in jail no more or nothing. We're taking you over to Geronimo and he'll deal with you."

"You bet," Ricardo agreed. "I bet you figured we'd both be drunk on our asses. That's why you tried to steal our truck."

"My truck," Eduardo corrected him. "They tried to steal *my* truck. And I ain't fuckin' drunk!"

"It don't make no difference *whose* truck they tried to rip off, dickhead!" Ricardo said. "And you're shit-faced." He looked over at Eduardo who now glared at him.

They both should have kept their eyes on Track.

Dan moved swiftly toward Eduardo on his right. His hand went under the shotgun barrel and flung it upward. The single-barreled weapon went off. Track droved his knuckles into the Apache's throat in a straight jab.

Eduardo, his trigger finger broken from the awkward way in which he'd been holding the shotgun when it went off, suffered even more physical damage from the blow. Blood spurted from his mouth and nose as his windpipe collapsed inward, a bleeding, bruising mass of tissue.

Steve, never one to let an opportunity slip by, moved almost simultaneously in a combination of sheer instinct and practice. He grabbed the Winchester and deftly pulled it from Ricardo's grasp. At the same time he spun on his right heel and drove his left elbow into his adversary's rib cage.

"Ooof!" Ricardo complained as a rib cracked under the impact. He staggered sideways, hurt but full of fight.

Steve now held the weapon's barrel with both hands. He raised it up and brought it down on Ricardo's head. A sound like that of a ripe watermelon splitting under a hot sun filled the air. Blood splattered out, then flowed heavily down his face. Ricardo, out cold, went down, landing on Eduardo who was on his hands and knees, vomiting into the sand.

Steve leaned down and said politely. "I presume the keys are in the truck?"

Eduardo, drunk and in shock, nodded before passing out.

13

Steve Aguila drove slowly up to the rear of the roadblock. The men there had dug a trench and reinforced it with sandbags. Several guards stood warily in firing position peering out into the night on the other side. Their friends, off duty but available in case of trouble, relaxed behind them around low campfires as they chatted quietly and drank coffee. All turned their gazes toward the sound of the truck as it neared them.

Steve kept the bright lights on, doing his best to approach the group of men straight on to force them to look directly into the high beams.

They squinted and one, more irritated than the others, yelled out, "Hey, dim them lights, man. You want to make us all blind or something?"

Then another, recognizing the truck, remarked sullenly, "It's the Culebras."

Dan Track, his natural white skin darkened by both the growth of beard and camouflage paint, kept the brim of his boonie hat turned down low over his face. Steve did the same, hoping that eyes torched by the headlights would not be able to see him plainly enough to make a positive identification.

"Did you guys come to join up with us?" someone shouted to the truck. "Or are you just driving around like you usually do?"

Steve made his voice low and gruff as he answered, "Up yours!" He turned the pickup sharply and drove rapidly away.

"I oughta put a bullet in the back o' that frigging truck cab," somebody said angrily. "Useless sons of bitches!"

Inside the vehicle, Track grinned sideways at Steve. "You better cool it. One of those guys might decide to settle an old score with the Culebras. Only you'd be the one paying the bill."

"I told you those two were unpopular," Steve said. He pressed his foot down hard on the accelerator. The finely tuned engine caught without a sputter, and the pickup raced out into open country.

They had visited no less than a half dozen positions located on the roads leading into the reservation. The conclusion they drew was unanimous. Llanero country was now effectively sealed off from the outside. Nobody was going to get in or out without a fight. That had been more than obvious at the barrier they'd seen just before this one. The shot-up police cars and the dead cop lying beside one of them had been easy to spot even across the highway.

"I wonder how long that dead cop's been lying out there," Track remarked.

"He's bloating up, so the body's been there since that firefight we heard a while back," Steve said. "And the fact the dead guy hasn't been removed shows there's a standoff going down."

"Did you notice those other dark spots on the road?" Track asked. "Looked like blood. They got whoever did that bleeding removed or med-evaced. That makes me think it was probably Apaches."

"Yeah," Steve said. "With the cop blown away, and outside pressure building up, the neutrals on the reservation are going to be forced to take sides whether they want to or not."

"Which side do you think they'll choose?" Track asked.

Steve shook his head sadly. "They're Llanero Apaches, man. They'll never turn against their own people in a conflict with strangers. You can already count them as part of Ferril's mob."

"That's what you told me back in San Diego," Track said. "Now I really feel flattered that you came to me for help. I didn't realize just how big a decision it was for you."

"Uh huh," Steve said. Then he looked at Track and displayed a wide grin. "I'm very discriminating when I ask somebody to die with me."

"I'm honored," Track said. "I'd hate like hell to be passed up for a good deal like that." He glanced around the area through the window. "We'd better shag ass," he suggested pointing at the pinkness of the rising sun dancing on the far horizon. "We won't be able to keep this up in daylight."

"Yeah," Steve agreed. "I just wish we knew for sure what was going on. We can only guess at this point. Other than the fact that there was a shoot-out between Llaneros and the state police, we don't know a thing."

"With that dead cop there, I'm sure the newspeople will be in on this," Track said.

"A lot of good that'll do us," Steve said. "I don't know if you've noticed it or not, but there's no newspaper delivery up to my stronghold."

"We don't need a newspaper," Track said. "And being at a high elevation will make reception that much easier."

"Reception?" Steve asked. "What the hell are you talking about?"

"This," Track said holding up a small transistor radio. "I found it under the seat." He switched it on and immediately picked up a Mexican radio station. Track twisted the dial several times until the clear tones of an American voice came over the air.

"What station did you pick up?" Steve said.

The radio announcer answered the question for him. "This is KXXL, Tucson, Arizona, the voice of the Sonoran Desert."

Track turned off the radio to save the batteries. "We are now part of the well-informed public."

ORV LINGENFELDER, who ran the small diner, could barely keep up with the orders that were brought to him by his newly hired waitresses. Sweating and frantic, he dipped baskets of sliced potatoes into hot oil and flipped hamburger patties two and three at a time on his grill.

Lingenfelder's sleepy business had blossomed into a real money-making operation since the legions of newsmen had descended on the police roadblock a couple of miles down the road. With no competition nearby, the journalists, some now dispeptic, had been forced to get their meals at the greasy spoon.

The diner operator had even been interviewed a couple of times by reporters desperate to send something—anything—back to their home offices. Lingenfelder, willing to lie to satisfy his customers and get himself plenty of attention, happily paraded out to appear in front of the cameras anytime he was asked.

At about the time Track and Steve had returned to the stronghold, Lingenfelder stood in front of his diner looking into the one-eyed glare of a TV camera. The early morning light was enhanced by spotlights and reflectors set up behind the little cafe.

The reporter, the same opportunist who had interviewed actress Myra Hawkins at the television special in Los Angeles, jumped straight into action with the question, "You were able to hear the battle between the state police and Apache Indians, were you not, Mr. Lingenfelder?"

"I sure was," Lingenfelder said. "It was a hell of—whoa! Can I say that on the TV?"

"Yes, sir," the reporter answered. "Please go on."

"Well, I could hear a big battle, you bet!"

"About how many shots did you hear, Mr. Lingenfelder?"

"Oh, hunnerds of 'em! Machine guns too!" Lingenfelder said. "And screams and crying of hurt folks!"

The reporter zeroed in to get the response he wanted. "Were any of those screams the voices of women and children?"

Even Lingenfelder hesitated at this point, but one more look at the camera encouraged him. "Uh—yeah! There was women—and kids—a bunch o' kids yelling—babies crying—ever'thing! It was awful!"

Other newsmen, particularly the foreigners who were standing by for their turn, could hardly wait to get at the diner operator. His picture would be transmitted into more than a million American and foreign homes as journalists plied him with the questions that would get the answers they sought. Answers that would catch the attention of a viewing audience already numbed by atrocities in Lebanon and Northern Ireland.

These TV reporters were hungry for news. While they had the spoken word of blood and gore, they had yet to produce one picture. And their patience was running out.

The sight of relief trucks moving in and out of police lines was of limited interest. It had begun to look like the entire story would fall apart for lack of any real action, when the answers to their prayers appeared a couple of hours after an uneventful sunrise.

A line of a dozen limousines arrived. Rented from a Tucson firm, they met the many flights that Courtney's pilot was making between Los Angeles and Sierra Vista. Among the passengers was Jerome Courtney himself—and he came with one of America's most popular TV actresses on his arm.

Ms Myra Hawkins was on the scene—and this time she was rehearsed, primed and ready for any necessary public statements.

And she wasted no time.

"I am here with Jerome to publicly declare my support for the Llanero Apache people," Ms Hawkins said. "And I also condemn the tactics of the Arizona State Police for their brutal massacre of innocent men, women and children." Her voice broke at this point, and her sincere regrets over the news she'd been given came through. "I—I cannot believe—that anyone could be capable of—such brutality—" She cried openly now, and turned to be embraced by Jerome Courtney.

"This is worse than Nazi Germany!" Courtney yelled. "But there will be justice!"

A voice from the crowd of reporters asked, "What's to be done, Mr. Courtney? And how are you involved?"

"The trucks that you see taking food and medicine onto the reservation are here through the efforts of a close friend of mine," Courtney said. "A man I admire and—"

"What's his name?"

"Who is he?"

Courtney loosened his grip somewhat on Ms Hawkins. "The gentleman wishes to remain anonymous. But I assure you that those big semis and their precious cargo are paid for by him and him alone."

The interview continued for several more minutes before another person caught the reporters' attention.

The second luxury auto produced a popular balladeer named Wayne Harrison. Dressed in his usual faded Levi's jacket and jeans, Harrison wasted no time in producing his worn guitar. Eager to bring the cameras to him as quickly as possible, he broke out into several protest songs that had made him famous during the late sixties and early seventies. Adored and idolized by a trendy, almost cultlike following, he was sure not only to bring a great deal of attention to the events on the Llanero Apache Reservation, but to also sway the opinion of a great percentage of the public to the side of the Indians.

He strolled up to Jerome Courtney and Myra Hawkins, his melodious voice singing a song of injustice in mines, lumber camps, farms and factories. With dark hair hanging to his shoulders, his sparking green eyes seemed to flash with each angry chord. The camera lights continued to stay lit as he launched into a special verse written for that particular happening:

"They say in the land of the Llanero,
Where justice has never shined—
That brave men and women have fallen
As the pigs' bullets whined!"

It wasn't good, but it was effective.

Jerome Courtney and Myra Hawkins, now joined by the other show-business people from the limousines, displayed their grief and anger by the silence of their furious expressions.

Standing by the roadblock, Officer Tim Turnbull trembled in rage and thought of his dead friend still lying out on that stinking highway.

AL PUGNACI CLAMPED an unlit stogie that had been smoked to the nub between his thick lips. He leaned against the semi and watched the Indians unload the food from inside it.

The driver, an old friend of his named Fish Pesco, put the flame of his lighter to a cigarette. He glanced at the Apaches. "Them's mean looking dudes, *compagno*."

Pugnaci laughed thickly. "You ain't wrong. And they're as tough as they look."

"They seem happy with the food," Pesco said.

"Yeah. They ain't got much out here. But I guess they'll have plenty when that guy Ferril gets things rolling."

"He's their *padrino*, eh? He looks meaner'n all of 'em put together." He spoke frankly, without fear. Pesco had leveled a weapon at more than one bad-ass in his day—and brought each and every one down too. It was more his habit of squandering his contract money than inefficiency that had forced him to resort to driving trucks and doing odd jobs in the illicit world he inhabited. "When's the plane due in?"

"Nobody tole you, huh?"

"No."

"They didn't tell you 'cause you ain't supposed to know," Pugnaci said. "You just stick close to me and I'll give you the word, okay?"

"Sure," Pesco said. "No sweat." He took no offence at his companion's remarks; need-to-know is the basis of security on both sides of the law. Pesco took another look around at the Indians. "What's them Injun broads like? You have one of 'em, Al?"

Pugnaci laughed. "If I ever do, I'll use your dick. I don't want mine cut off."

Pesco was silent for a few moments before speaking again. "This place gives me the creeps. I'll be glad when the plane gets here."

WITH FAMOUS PEOPLE now in the area, some of the locals began to make appearances to see the show along the police barricades. The scene became like a carnival with the spectators laughing, talking and excitedly pointing at celebrities they recognized.

The biggest event of the day came in the late afternoon of that same day. Not only did more show biz folks make appearances in rented limousines after plane rides from Los Angeles aboard Sherman's Lear jet, but Senator Ted O'Connor came in via an air force helicopter from Williams Air Force Base near Mesa, Arizona.

He disembarked from the aircraft to a flurry of appreciative comments from both the famous and the common people in the crowd. He waved and smiled only slightly, his concern and anger evident from the way he knifed through the crowd to greet his old friend Jerome Courtney.

The journalists crowded around. "Any statements, Senator?" several called out.

"Yes," O'Connor answered. He motioned the people to silence. "I've been appointed by the president as his special representative in this matter. The first order—"

"What is the official version of what happened?" someone cried out.

O'Connor again signaled for quiet. "The first order of business is to see that the Indians are out of danger. Arrangements have to be made for me to meet with several of their representatives."

"Will we be allowed—"

"No news coverage at that point," interrupted O'Connor. "I shall visit the reservation at a time yet to be arranged. Until then, ladies and gentlemen of the press, no statements."

The good senator did, however, agree to pose for some shots on one of the trucks carrying supplies onto the reservation.

A mile on the other side of the diner, off on a sideroad, Trevor Levant relaxed in a large, air-conditioned RV. He'd had it brought in for his use with the first truck convoy. It held every possible luxury that a man of his tastes could expect in what he considered primitive surroundings.

Outside, several armed men were stationed for security, while another sat in silence in the driver's seat keeping a watch through the large windshield.

A CB radio, turned on but silent, sat by Levant's elbow as he sipped an iced tea. Suddenly a voice he recognized as Pugnaci's sounded over a speaker. "The tank is full. The tank is full," the mobster said using their prearranged code.

Levant smiled and picked up the microphone. He pressed the transmit button. "Start the engine—I say again—start the engine!"

14

Once again it was sneak-and-peak time for Dan Track and Steve Aguila.

The two stripped for silent movement carrying only the bare essentials. No excess gear or paraphernalia hung on the web belts around their waists. Besides ammo bandoliers, they each carried only a single canteen in case of an emergency that might leave them stranded out in the desert during daylight hours, and Buckmaster survival knives that Steve had conveniently provided for them. They left the slings of the M-16 rifles behind in the base camp. The sling-swivels had been taped down to keep them from rattling against the weapons as their owners went about the deadly business of poking around where unfriendly personnel were waiting to blow them away.

The pair had come down from Steve's stronghold for one reason: to investigate the arrival and quick departure of a light, twin-engine aircraft earlier that same evening at sunset.

The plane, easily heard up in the mountains, had been flying low without navigation lights. A series of low flames on the horizon showed Track and Steve that a clandestine, temporary landing strip had been set up somewhere on the reservation. The small fires they had observed could be nothing else but smudge-pot lights to guide the airplane in for a safe landing. It had remained on the ground for only fifteen minutes before its idling engines roared back to life, its props pulling the machine back into the air to return south.

Track and Steve had taken all this in from their hidden base camp. After the plane had disappeared and its engines could no longer be heard, Track asked, "What's that bastard bringing in?"

Steve shrugged. "Maybe they're speeding up the food shipments."

Track shook his head. "No way. According to the newscasts, there's been a truck coming into the reservation once a day, and sometimes twice. You'd think they'd have plenty of supplies by now."

"The plane came from Mexico, Dan," Steve said.

"Mmm," Track said rubbing the thickening beard on his chin, "arms and ammo. Maybe even additional personnel. Do you think that's what's going on?"

"Additional personnel? I doubt it. They'd only bring in more Llanero Apaches, but there's no other tribal reservation, so that's out of the question," Steve said.

"Maybe it's just one guy," Track suggested. "Could be somebody who went to the outside world for some reason or other. Maybe even some rich Apache who left the reservation years ago for the good life and now, having seen what's going on in the television news, has decided to come back and rejoin the tribe."

"Sounds logical," Steve said. "Or maybe some of those TV actors have come in for a visit or something."

"That's a real possibility. If so, that fucking Geronimo Ferril is pulling the propaganda con job of the century." Track said. "Ol' Joseph Goebbels is probably rolling over in his grave right now."

"Hell, Dan! We're only guessing here." Steve's voice was bitter. "I'm interested in bringing murder charges against Ferril and his top dogs. If finding out about that airplane will speed things up, then I'm ready to pussyfoot out there and have a look around."

Track had looked up and studied the quickly darkening sky. "About an hour more." After preparing themselves, they had settled down to wait for the conditions of darkness to be just right.

Now, the desert locked in by the night, Track and Steve followed every dip in the ground and shadows cast by the rolling terrain. Traveling slowly and cautiously, they approached the spot where they estimated the crude landing field had been laid out.

Steve, a few paces ahead, suddenly held up his hand and dropped it. He went to the ground in a silent dive; Track took his cue.

The sounds were soft. To a casual camper or a careless, inattentive scout, they would not have been audible at all. But to keen ears, they were as loud as bugle blasts.

Footsteps ahead in the desert sand—approaching.

Track signaled Steve to remain stationery. Then he crawled over to his right to a small mound that flowed up from the flatter area. His positioning would put the approaching strangers directly between him and Steve.

Five minutes later three men, barely silhouetted against the lighter sky, came into view. The trio moved catlike, yet still were a bit careless in their ignorance of the impending trouble directly in front of them.

Steve recognized the lead man. It was one of Ferril's most loyal followers, a son of a bitch who Steve knew had offed at least two of his reservation cops. Steve, using a night aiming technique, pointed his weapon toward the patrol, peering over the top of the muzzle. He fired, his bullet striking under the man's chin and lifting him a foot off the ground.

Track, afraid the third would try a getaway, got in a body shot that spun his human target around. The guy's legs collapsed and he flopped to the sand.

The second man dove behind the first's body, wasting no time with preliminaries. Semi-automatic fire filled the silent vacuum left by the cessation of fire of Track and Steve's M-16s.

The sound of the weapon brought a chill to both ambushers, and they could identify it immediately through past experience—it was an AK-47.

"Just like the fucking Charlies!" Steve gasped involuntarily.

More rounds kicked up around the two as their adversary changed to full-automatic. After each fusillade, the guy moved back covering his own withdrawal.

Steve, lower than Track, rose up for a better sighting, but the movement brought unwanted attention in the form of a swarm of 7.62 mm bullets that forced him back down.

Damn, take it easy—that son of a bitch knows what he's doing! Steve thought.

Track's M-16 barked on full-auto now. The rounds were fired quickly, not so much with the intention of hitting the man, but more with the idea of putting a stop to the retrograde movements that might lead to the bastard's escape.

Steve's rifle exploded with several quick shots. Track leaped to his feet at the same time and rushed parallel to the enemy's position. He managed to get ten paces before he was forced back to the ground by a shower of bullets.

Steve leaped up and cut loose again, then dropped back to the sand. Although he'd only taken a quick look, he could recognize the man from his build and the curious way he wore his Stetson pushed back on his head. A wild spray of bullets flew over his head. Steve waited a beat then shouted, "Give it up, Raul."

Raul Venida didn't answer.

"You're cut off, man," Steve said. "Raise the *manos*, brother."

"I ain't your brother, you asshole!" Venida yelled back.

"Where'd you get the AK-47?" Steve asked.

Venida didn't answer, but he fired out toward Track's position. "Stay where you are, fucker!"

Steve fired again. "You're not going anywhere, man!"

Track, forcing himself into the dirt, did the low crawl in an attempt to maneuver to a better position. Once again dirt flew and the air buzzed in concert with Venida's spitting assault rifle.

Steve sprayed out a volley of 5.56 slugs, and Track moved again.

"You motherfuckers!" Venida screamed. "You ain't got a chance!" He pumped a storm of bullets toward Steve, then swung the muzzle to where he thought Track was, to put out another curtain of lead. Then he leaped to his feet, turned and headed back toward safety.

Track, now positioned directly in front of him, fired one round.

It smashed through Venido's teeth, threw his nose off to one side and popped both eyeballs out of their sockets before bursting out the top of his skull. The Apache flopped down on his ass, and rolled to one side.

Both Track and Steve warily approached the corpse. Venido lay in an untidy heap. Track paid him the ultimate compliment. "He was a bad-assed dude."

"That he was," Steve said. "And a rotten son of a bitch when he wanted to be. He was a backshooter."

"With balls though," Track added. "He didn't turn chicken against the two of us."

A round suddenly zapped between them, and both Track and Steve were hugging terra firma in blind, instinctive dives.

Two more salvos roared over their heads.

"Shit!" Track complained. "Does everybody in the fucking world own a fucking AK-47?"

"Everybody in this part of the world seems to," Steve said. "Looks like we ambushed the point men of a bigger patrol."

"Time to fire and maneuver," Track said. "Take off."

"Say no more!" Steve, crawling low, moved away from the source of fire while Track cranked out several showers of steel. Then Steve, shooting perilously close to his friend, gave him the opportunity to move back to join him.

The fire and maneuver continued without pause for the next ten minutes. Then a fresh burst of fire from their flanks brought the pair to a halt.

Several long streams of bullets played over them and kicked up dust a few scant yards away. It was only a matter of a minute or more before the sprays would punch into them.

"Shit!" Steve swore. "We're outflanked!"

"You know what we gotta do?"

"Yeah," Steve said. The answer was obvious. The only choicc they had was to break through before they were completely surrounded. Their prospects of success were practically nil, but that was the choice. Steve wet his lips and asked, "Which side do we charge?"

Track pointed in the direction of the stronghold. "That's the way home."

"Let's do it!" Steve said.

"Right. When I say 'go,' got it?"

"Yo!"

"One more thing," Track said.

"What's that?" Steve asked.

"Don't take any prisoners."

Steve laughed. "You crazy bastard!"

"Go!"

OFFICER TURNBULL STOOD in the bright lights around the police roadblock. Outside this illuminated circle was complete blackness. Back on duty after a twelve-hour break, he was freshly shaved and rested, standing tall in a clean and pressed uniform.

Senator Ted O'Connor and Jerome Courtney stood at the sawhorses that were sitting end-to-end across the highway. Behind them were Myra Hawkins and Wayne Harrison with a couple of lesser show business lights who played supporting roles in the same series that Myra starred in.

Off to both sides, carefully positioned through their own arrangements, the inevitable TV newsmen and camera crews were poised to begin recording the event that had been arranged earlier in the day. The media, finally growing tired of jostling and fighting each other, had made an agreement to conduct themselves in a manner to give all a chance to effectively cover the story.

Tourists and visiting locals had their own cameras recording events for photo albums and to show the folks back home after vacation. The number of popping flashbulbs attested to the crowd's large size.

Turnbull turned his glance to his left where the approach of several spokesmen for the Llanero Apaches were expected to materialize at any time.

"Assholes," Turnbull said softly.

"What's that?" the cop next to him, a young guy named Perez, asked.

"I said, 'assholes,'" Turnbull reiterated.

"Make that with a capital 'A,'" Perez added.

A few moments before, after several bursts of gunfire had been heard in the direction of the reservation, Jerome Courtney had turned nasty. He'd broken into screaming accusations of police brutality. According to him the law was carrying on a massacre of the Indians at the same moment they waited for them to appear for a parley. The captain in charge of the roadblock had tried to assure the distraught man that nothing of the sort was going on. It had taken Senator O'Connor a quarter of an hour to calm Courtney. And even then, it had been necessary for Myra Hawkins to aid in talking him down from his rage.

Turnbull stared holes into Courtney now. The TV producer, sensing the unfriendly vibrations coming his way, had turned to face him. The two locked eyes in a staring contest until a slight commotion broke out in the darkness in the direction of the reservation.

Within a few moments three Apache Indians walked into the circle of light thrown out by the barricade's illumination system. They did not wear the usual western-style modern dress associated with Arizona Indians. They were dressed in buckskin vests, breechcloths, high moccasins, and brightly colored headbands.

Turnbull noted they carried no weapons.

Two of the Apaches came to a halt, while a third continued forward for five yards. He raised his hand. "I want to speak to Senator O'Connor and Mr. Courtney."

The police captain motioned to Turnbull and Perez. They walked to the barricades and removed one of the sawhorses. Both O'Connor and Courtney stepped through the opening and approached the Indian.

"I am Lobo," the man said, "Wolf in your language."

"How do you do, Mr. er—Wolf," the Senator said offering his hand. "I am Senator—well, that is to say, my name is Ted."

Lobo ignored the offered hand. He looked at Courtney. "And you?"

"Jerome—Jerry," Courtney said thrilled to be speaking to a bona fide Indian warrior.

"Yes, we know of you," Lobo said. "Around the Llanero council fires, we call you Good Friend. To us, that is your name."

"Thank you," Courtney said almost delirious with happiness.

O'Connor, a bit miffed that there was no special name for him mentioned with all those cameras rolling, wasted no time. "Are you the spokesperson for the Llanero Apache Reservation?"

"No," Lobo snapped. "I am not the spokes*man* for the Llanero Apache Tribe. Our chief is Geronimo, and he has sent me to inform you that he will issue a public statement at noon, day after tomorrow."

"Is there anything you need?" Courtney asked. "Have you received the food we've sent in?"

"Yes," Lobo said.

More gunfire sounded.

"What the hell was that?" O'Connor exclaimed.

Lobo ignored him. "Geronimo will expect full television coverage of his statement." He raised his voice to make sure the newspeople could hear. "He will answer no questions, nor tolerate anyone who tries to ask him any. Is that understood?"

"Yes. Yes, of course," O'Connor said. "Who is Geronimo?"

"Their leader," Courtney said answering the question. "I am acquainted with him through a very close friend. I'll explain more to you later." He turned to Lobo. "Geronimo can trust us," he assured the Apache.

Several short bursts of automatic firing sounded in the far distance.

"Are there soldiers or police shooting your people?" Courtney wanted to know. "You can tell us."

"I have nothing to say," Lobo said stonily. Inwardly he knew that Steve Aguila and the stranger with him were no doubt heavily engaged in combat against a Llanero war party. He desperately hoped that the problem with the interlopers was being solved at that very moment. He kept his face passive as he continued to speak to the senator and the television producer. "Remember. Noon, day after tomorrow, you will be given a statement by Geronimo. No interviews or press conferences—just a simple statement." He turned and walked back to his escorts.

More bursts of gunfire could be heard.

The Apaches hurried away into the darkness.

15

Muzzle flashes sparked in brief flares of light while the deafening reports of weapons roared across the gentle slope of the desert floor.

Running slightly uphill, Track and Steve had changed from defence maneuvers to attack. They swung their weapons back and forth in overlapping fields of fire, pumping a heavy spray of bullets like a shield in front of them. Most of this skillful fire served to force their adversaries' heads down, but the pair were also rewarded twice with the sight of individual Llaneros kicked over to die in the steel storm they hosed at them.

A heavy volume of fire during a maneuvering or charging phase is the key to making the movement a success. It also guarantees a reasonable chance of survival to those who are shagging their asses through or toward enemy positions. This gave Track and Steve a good advantage at that particular time. Their individual locations, while visible only in pulsating muzzle flashes, were constantly changing, which made them elusive targets.

Despite this advantage, a chance shot did some damage. Track's hat spun off his head and he felt what seemed to be a stinging blow to the side of his head. He staggered and tripped, feeling the hot flow of blood run out of his hair and down behind his right ear and soaking into his collar.

"Track?" Steve hesitated, but kept up his volume of fire.

"Let's go!" Track recovered quickly, regaining his feet and continuing to charge.

A determined Apache, cool enough to assume a kneeling position, loomed up in front of them. He aimed carefully through the aligned front and rear sights.

Track veered left, Steve to the right, then zigzagged twice.

The Indian wavered, trying to get a good sight in the flashing, intermittent light. Then he attempted to change targets, and tried it again.

Steve was more decisive.

The unfriendly crumpled under the impact of a belly shot from Steve's weapon. Gasping for breath, he raised up and took a round from Track in the throat that sent a fountain of blood spurting from his mouth. The third shot, quickly snapped off by Steve, hit the shoulder and tore through the heart.

This was the last defender. Track led them for another fifteen yards, then found a shallow gully that had been washed into the earth by winter rains. He dove into it, then turned to fight off the expected counterattack.

Steve joined him. The moon was out of the clouds by then, and Track's bloody head was visible. Steve was concerned. "You okay, buddy?"

Track touched the wound. His gingerly probing fingers found no serious damage. "Must have been a ricochet off a rock," he said in a hoarse whisper. "It smacked me enough to break the skin and trip me up. I'm okay."

"Way to go," Steve said. "Whoops! Here they come—the bastards!"

"Stay quiet," Track urged him.

The two made no moves, but listened intently to the cautiously approaching patrol. Whoever was the patrol leader gave short, terse orders in whispers. He was unable to use hand and arm signals in the darkness. Spread out, the Apaches unknowingly walked past their quarry, continuing slowly out into the desert.

The clouds, thick and deep that night, continued to glide across the sky. A brief opening gave Track and his companion a chance to look at their gradually departing enemy. "The fuckers are wearing fatigues—foreign pattern," Steve said.

"Probably came in with those AK-47s," Track said. He studied the uniforms until the clouds once again closed in on the yellow orb of the moon. "Czechoslovakian camouflage, I'd say."

"Oh, shit! They're coming back," Steve interrupted.

Track silently congratulated the bad guys for a good move. If there had been a successful escape, then there was no chance of catching anyone. But if the two attackers were still in the area, they just might make contact.

The moon came out again, making the latter possible.

"Goddamn it!" Track said. He and Steve pumped their M-16s into the surprised patrol. The two leading Apaches crumpled under the volley. Their companions wisely hit the dirt.

Track and Steve each cranked out a second, shorter fusillade, then turned and hauled ass in the opposite direction. The air around their heads sang with passing bullets. A nearby barrel cactus had chunks torn from its green trunk, wet pulp spraying out in a wide splash that hit both Track and Steve.

Once again the two were in the darkness. Being the hunted gave them the same advantage they'd enjoyed before. They went to ground to await developments.

The patrol, spread out in a long skirmish line, was forced to cover as much territory as possible. Unable to pinpoint their targets, they could only hope to stumble across them or, at worst, come under fire in order to locate the two elusive evaders.

Track, lying concealed in the shadow of the same cactus that had blasted them, was out of sight to Steve. The Apache policeman had found cover behind a small rock formation that rose a half foot from the ground.

"Cover the left!" came the whispered voice of the patrol leader.

"It's covered," someone assured him. "Tortuga and Camisa are out that direction."

The sweat trickling down Track's face was now as much the result of nervousness as exertion. He couldn't estimate exactly, but he knew he was down to no more than two or three rounds in the magazine of the M-16. There was no way he could reload without attracting attention to himself. If he was forced to fire, he'd be outgunned within a couple of trigger pulls.

The same thing would happen if Steve was discovered.

Track slowly but steadily eased his hand toward the shoulder holster that held the Beretta. The range and darkness would make a close-packed battlefield. Perfect for a skilled pistoleer like himself.

But the patrol continued past them.

A half hour later, Track quietly joined his buddy. "They'll be back, but I think they're going to make some wide sweeps. If they keep falling into ambushes, none of 'em will be alive by daylight."

"That patrol leader knows it too," Steve said.

"Sons of bitches!" Track said. "They'll stick around though. We'll have to check out that landing strip tomorrow night."

"I agree," Steve said. "There'll be more of 'em in another couple of hours. I just want to know if that order of yours not to take prisoners still stands."

"The only exceptions will be good-looking women who clearly show they have the brains and the morals of alley cats," Track said. He patted Steve's shoulder. "Let's go home. There's not much more we can do tonight."

The two moved out across the open country toward the Caballo Mountains, putting distance between themselves and the patrol who still cautiously searched for them in the darkness.

16

The exciting events on the Llanero Apache Reservation caught the world's attention like nothing else, short of total war.

The Communist bloc nations were delighted with the grist the situation provided for their anti-American propaganda mill. Russians, Poles, Bulgarians, Hungarians, *et al.*, were treated to news accounts that told of courageous Indians being ground under the boot heels of American paratroopers and marines. Fidel Castro spent four solid hours on *La Television Cubana* blasting everything Yankee—from the capitalist system itself right down to such bourgeoise delights as rock music and X-rated movies. He warned his populace that the brutal subjugation of the Indian reservation was only one part of a gigantic plan of American imperialism.

The news versions given to the free world weren't much more accurate, but no mention was made of a plot to conquer the world. The populations of the western democracies were focusing nearly all their attention on the situation. They clamored for more news of the Llanero Apache rebellion. Even European antinuclear groups paused in their demonstrations at various missile bases to travel to the streets of several cities on the continent to announce their support for the Indians in several noisy rallies.

American college students found the situation with the Apache Indians even more to their liking than the events in Central America or South Africa. This was not only closer to home, but it was an event pointing out misdeeds and grievances that could be laid heavily on the older generations. Most were content with picketing and chanting slogans, but the demonstrators at Cal Berkely thought it a perfect opportunity to occupy several campus buildings. They were at a loss to explain how this was to be effective in dealing with the mistreatment of Apache Indians since the university had absolutely no connection with the problem. Nothing serious in the way of damage was caused, and there were no arrests. In fact, it all turned out to be rather good fun in the end, although a couple of rowdies managed to attract a bit of attention with a spasm of rock throwing. This didn't amount to much, however, and the demonstration came to a gradual and peaceful halt early in the evening. There were classes the next day, and a lot of the young people had some serious studying to catch up on.

There were even a few somewhat sedate gatherings of students at a couple of small Christian colleges in the south. They supported the Indians with fund drives, raising a rather impressive sum that was properly forwarded to the Bureau of Indian Affairs in Washington. After all, these religious youths were firm supporters of the American Way, and the underdog had always received the cheers of God-fearing Americans.

There were still large holes in the news stories from the Llanero reservation, which had to be plugged. Newspapers and magazines produced dozens of hastily written stories that purported to tell all, but really told nothing. Most of these were written by journalists who dug into the rather skimpy histories of the Llanero tribe to produce stories of minor literary merit and newsworthiness. When they'd gone to this particular well several times too often, they turned to the stories of the numerous Apache peoples and produced column after column until the reading public set up a collective groan.

The television news folks had it slightly better.

Old film footage that stereotyped Indians, served to show that the country's population at large had always been ignorant about native Americans. The usual breast beating followed as people looked for causes, and other spontaneous supporters spouted their outrage. But after a while even this began to die off.

Then the news folks got a break.

Roberto Lobo made another appearance. As before, he met the crowd of reporters and celebrities at the police roadblock. Dressed in authentic Apache regalia and sporting war paint this time. Although he was still weaponless, he looked tough and menacing nevertheless.

Lobo's first announcement was met with expressions of chagrin by the journalists. "Our chief, Geronimo, has postponed his news conference for twenty-four hours."

Expressions of anger and impatience caused one of the reporters to be unusually direct. "Hey!" he shouted testily. "We aren't going to keep you people in the headlines forever! You'd better tell Geronimo to show up and do it fast!"

"Yeah!" another agreed. "We need copy and plenty of it!"

"Give us something to show the people!" a TV reporter urged.

Lobo's temper flashed, but he controlled his emotions. He had been advised to expect the reaction he got. Geronimo Ferril was playing a teasing game, and had told him that the press publicity potential was going to be milked until it ran dry.

It was now time to tease a bit.

"Geronimo has consented to allow four particular people to visit the reservation with one of the 'mercy trucks.' Those folks are considered good friends of the Llanero Apache tribe."

"What networks do they belong to?" a reporter hollered.

"None," Lobo said. "I'm officially inviting Mr. Jerome Courtney, Senator Ted O'Connor, Mr. Wayne Harrison and Miss Myra Hawkins to pay a call on our people."

The quartet, who had been standing to the side with a police escort, hurried forward. "Thank you! Thank you!" Courtney said happily. "We're honored. We truly are!"

"What an opportuntity," Ms Hawkins said clapping her hands together.

"This is an opportunity to get into some serious and meaningful dialogue," the senator said loud enough to make sure the TV cameras picked him up. "There's a good chance we can reach a peaceful resolution to a situation that is threatening to blow sky-high at any moment."

"I'll write a song that'll tear people's hearts out," Harrison promised.

The angry reporter was furious. He glanced at Lobo. "You're putting your thanks in the wrong corner. If we decide to ignore you Indians, you and your whole damn cause'll go down the public toilet—forgotten forever!"

Lobo smiled, ignoring the outburst as if it wasn't worthy of his attention. "There'll also be a half dozen television reporters with their cameramen allowed to accompany that same truck onto the reservation. These people will—"

"Goddamn it!" a member of the press corps shouted. "What about us magazine and newspaper guys?"

A television reporter guffawed. "Get it on the six o'clock news, asshole!"

"You son of a bitch!" The magazine man charged at the TV guy with the big mouth.

Officers Tim Turnbull and Carlos Perez bulled their way into the swarming people. They pulled the two combatants apart and pushed them away from each other. "One more outbreak and there'll be arrests!" Turnbull threatened. "It's bad enough around here without you dickheads starting trouble on this side of the barricade."

The two scrappers, not really wanting to mix it up, treated each other to surly scowls, but made no further attempts to throttle each other.

Lobo spoke again after things quieted down. "Like I was saying, there'll be six TV reporters with cameramen allowed to come onto the reservation on a mercy truck."

"That's me!" an eager reporter shouted.

"Hold it, goddamn it!" Lobo shouted. "*I'm* in charge here!" The instincts of a Marine drill instructor—which he'd been for two years—came to the fore. "You'll come forward as I call out your stations. Those that are chosen will stand over to the side of the road there, until directed onto a vehicle." He paused and glared at them, his eyes blazing through the war paint. "Any questions?"

There were none.

"All right. We'll have ABC, CBS, NBC, CNN, the BBC and Japanese National Television." He gave them another withering stare. "Now, goddamn it! *Move!*"

The reporters not called out were disappointed, but realized they had no recourse. Any further displays of outrage on their part could mean they would never be admitted onto the reservation. They stayed quiet while the lucky ones, either pulling or pushing their cameramen, rushed across the road to the spot indicated.

"Hold it!" Lobo shouted. He walked over to the NBC team. He looked at the woman reporter who stood with her assistant. "No women. It won't be permitted!"

The young woman was properly incensed. "I beg your pardon! My credentials—"

Lobo sneered. "Llanero custom is strict about the role of women in society—*our* society."

An anxious man from the crowd hollered out. "Let me take her place, okay?"

The woman turned. "Fuck off, buster!" She pointed at Myra Hawkins. "What about the actress over there?"

"She's special," Lobo said coldly. "Her heart's in the right place."

The woman didn't want to keep her network from getting a good story. She beckoned to a young male who was part of NBC's entourage standing by the police. "Let's go, Buddy."

The kid, barely out of journalism school, hurried across to her. "I'll do my best."

"You damned well better!" the woman said. Infuriated, she looked up into Lobo's face. "Your own women will be clamoring for their freedom from chauvinists like you."

Lobo grabbed her arm and hustled her toward the barricade so fast her feet barely hit the ground. After picking her up and setting her down on the other side of the sawhorses, he grinned. "And you now know how we handle mouthy broads." He walked over to the others. "Wait here for the truck. We've got a pickup for you."

Myra Hawkins, now suddenly furious, started to join the woman reporter, but Courtney grabbed her arm. Myra tried to pull free. "I'm not going with that son of a bitch!"

"Shhh!" Courtney begged her. "You should be honored. This is a special acknowledgment of your worth to the Llanero people."

Myra reluctantly calmed down. "Well... all right." But she cast a sincerely sympathetic look at the woman who angrily stood with her network people behind the barricade.

TRACK SWITCHED OFF THE RADIO and put it into his backpack. "That guy pushed that woman around in front of cameras. Wonder what the public is going to think of that."

"It'll probably make their basic philosophies turn a flip-flop," Steve said. "A woman mistreated, but by a minority revolutionary."

"Most folks won't know whether to hate him or not," Track said. "But I suppose Ferril isn't that worried about philosophies."

"I know Roberto Lobo quite well," Steve said. "He really sounded like himself over the radio. If there was ever a guy to proudly wear the title of chauvinist, it's him."

"Damn!" Track said, "I'm starting to get that old Vietnam feeling again," he remarked.

"Because of those AK-47s?" Steve asked. He sat a couple of yards away, leaning comfortably against a rock sipping hot coffee from a canteen cup.

"Yeah," Track answered, "that, and the fact that a big portion of the American public seems to be rooting for the guys I'm fighting against."

Steve nodded. "Yeah. It's possible that fucking Ferril could come out of this a folk hero. If we don't show him up for what he is, we'll go down with the reputation of being a couple of mindless thugs."

Track poured some hot water into his own cup. After stirring in some field-ration coffee, he settled back. "There's only one way to avoid any infamy as well as jail."

"Jail!" Steve remarked.

"Hell, yes," Track said. "We've been offing guys around here for the past few weeks, Steve. It's going to be our word against a whole Indian tribe if we get policed up."

"Of course if we're dead, we won't care much what they say about us."

"I don't like to think that negatively," Track said. "Deep inside here—" he smacked his belly hard with his fist "—I've got a gut feeling that Geronimo Ferril isn't really doing much more than pulling a criminal scam. All this talk about fighting discrimination and mistreatment is a bunch of bullshit on his part. I don't think he gives a damn about that."

"Hell!" Steve snorted. "I *know* he doesn't."

"Then when we walk off this reservation we'd better damned well have plenty of proof to back up our allegations," Track said.

"Then let's go get it," Steve urged him. "Hell, we know there's some shady shit going down with those airplanes and trucks over at that landing strip."

"That's going all the way," Track said. "We'll be able to make only one more trip in that direction. We'll either pull a coup, or Geronimo Ferril will piss on our graves."

Steve didn't hesitate. "It's worth it for me."

"And to me," Track said. "I suggest we get ready for it. And I mean more than just slapping camouflage grease on our faces and taping down the M-16s."

"You're talking spiritually, right?"

"Right. I want to pull back into myself and draw out all the reserves of energy and concentration I've got there," Track said.

"I'm an Indian," Steve said. "An Apache Indian. I have my way of preparing for a showdown, and especially one that just might be the final one of my life."

Track, a *karateka* with a fourth degree black belt in Tai Kwon Do, would use his own mental and spiritual meditative ways. "Tomorrow night," he said calmly, "we make the big move."

Steve smiled without humor. "A good day to die."

THE APACHE GUARDS at the roadblock deftly swung open the gate that blocked the main entrance into the Llanero reservation.

A small convoy passed through the opening, the people in it waving to the warriors standing there. The first vehicle was a Willys jeep in which Roberto Lobo and his friend Ricardo Pantera rode. Pantera drove while Lobo sat in the front passenger's seat keeping a close eye on the people following them.

The second conveyance was a limousine driven by Al Pugnaci. His passengers were Jerome Courtney, Senator Ted O'Connor, Myra Hawkins and Wayne Harrison. These three, sitting in the air-conditioned interior, were all smiles. They gave the "V" peace sign to the Indian men standing guard at the barricade. A couple of the Apaches, veterans of Vietnam, were tempted to shoot back the well-known "bird," but Geronimo Ferril's instructions had been plain: they were to be courteous and friendly to all visitors.

Behind the limousine, dusty and uncomfortable in the back of an Apache-owned pickup truck with upright stake sides, sat the newspeople. These were professionals, however, several of whom had been on dangerous assignments in war. The cameramen didn't let an opportunity slip by as they swept the area with their lenses.

The final vehicle was a semitrailer driven by Fish Pesco. He'd made plenty of trips into the reservation and knew exactly where he was going. Al Pugnaci had also seen to it that he was well drilled in what would be expected of him in front of the journalists and celebrities.

Pantera stopped the Willys and Lobo jumped down. He beckoned everyone to leave their vehicles and join him. When all had gathered around, he pointed to several large spots on the macadam of the main highway. "Those are blood spots left by two of our people who were gunned down by the police!" he shouted. "They became martyrs on that terrible day. This isn't propaganda, this is human blood!" Lobo motioned to the newspeople. "I want—I *demand*—to see that on the six o'clock news!"

He waited until they'd all turned their cameras on the area indicated before motioning everyone back into the vehicles. Then the convoy continued.

Lobo failed to point out where a dead policeman and three shot-up Arizona State Police cars had been situated before finally being moved out of sight. The dead man had been buried in the bottom of a desert ravine. Then the autos had been pushed over the edge to crash down on top of his grave.

The caravan continued down the dusty road for another five miles before they reached an encampment of wickiups. A crowd of women and children shouted enthusiastic greetings and surged forward when the vehicles came to a halt.

Pesco stepped down from his cab and walked to the back of the truck to open the trailer. The people immediately formed into a line that was as orderly as it was well rehearsed.

Lobo strode over to the limousine where Courtney, O'Connor, Myra Hawkins and Harrison now stood. The Apache greeted them with a nod, then pointed to the line of women and kids. "The hungry little ones are going to get their food. Many of them have lost their men to the guns of the fascist police. They have no one to provide for them but the tribe—and you good people."

"How sad!" Myrna exclaimed. She spotted a chubby little boy standing beside his mother. "The poor little tyke!" She started to go over to the toddler, but Lobo grabbed her arm. The actress looked up at him with imploring eyes. "Oh, please. I must hold him! Love him! Comfort him!"

"We are a proud people," Lobo said. "It's bad enough we must take food from outsiders. To be coddled—especially for a man-child—would be the same as an insult."

"Love never hurt anyone!" Myra snapped.

"Please, Myra," the senator said intervening. "We mustn't clash with their culture."

"Very well," Myra said. "I certainly didn't mean to offend. I'm so sorry."

Courtney slipped an arm around her. "It's all right, darling. We all feel the same."

Wayne Harrison spoke up, "We certainly do!" He quickly got his guitar out of the car. "Surely they can't object to a song," he said to Lobo.

"Help yourself, man," the Apache said.

Harrison broke into "John Henry" and when that ended, took up with "Old Judge Parker Take Your Shackles Off of Me." He followed this with the protest singer Woody Guthrie's more famous "This Land Is Your Land."

The Apache Indians, who didn't consider the land theirs *and* anybody else's as the song suggested—and would have preferred Billy Joel or Linda Rondstat—listened politely nevertheless.

The cameras kept humming as Roberto Lobo produced people for interviews. A couple of warriors, but mostly women and a couple of half-grown children, cleverly recited the lines that had been written for them by Geronimo Ferril.

Meanwhile, the food and clothing brought in on Pesco's truck was duly issued out. Myra Hawkins was finally allowed to hold an Indian child in her arms. The image, taped by all cameras, would appear across the world on millions of television sets.

The session wound down, finally ending with a firm announcement by Roberto Lobo. "Tomorrow, at noon without fail, our leader, Geronimo, will appear at the police roadblock for a press conference." He paused. "Now, I thank you for visiting us, and must ask you to return to your vehicles for the trip back. Thank you. Thank you all."

Now more determined than ever to back up the Indian rebellion, Courtney and his small entourage returned to their limousine. The newsmen, happily in possession of solid material to broadcast to the world hungry for a look inside the Llanero reservation, stormed to the pickup truck and clamored aboard loudly and excitedly.

Fish Pesco watched them drive back down the road. Then he went to his truck and swung back up into the cab. Now that he'd made a delivery, he had some stuff to pick up over at the landing strip.

17

George Beegh hit the brakes of the Ford Bronco, kicking up clouds of dust as he came to an abrupt halt in front of the rural mail box. He climbed wearily out of the cab. His fatigue wasn't so much from the trip he'd just made up from Albuquerque as from the two nights he'd spent doing the nightlife of that New Mexico city.

But George's visit hadn't been simply for long hours of revelry. The real reason sat in a nylon and leather guncase on the seat of the truck: a brand spanking new, Colt AR-15 9 mm semiautomatic beauty of a carbine. This was one first he wanted to score on his uncle Dan Track. While his "old man" was away, George planned not only to give it a thorough and painstaking test but also to write up the results and get them published. For once he could do the talking and Track could do the listening.

George flipped open the mailbox and dragged out a few circulars and bills. There was nothing interesting—no letters from a gun publication or any "Wish you were here" postcards from Track telling his nephew about his visit in San Diego. George really wanted to know when he was coming back so he'd be able to get the AR-15 tested and written up before Track's return.

He climbed back into the truck then drove up the road past the mailbox to the house set deep into the red hills. This was where he lived with his Uncle Dan, their housekeeper, and a cat named Dorothy.

After pulling up in front of the garage, George grabbed his valise and the gun case, then climbed out of the truck and walked up to the front door. Their cat, lying indolently in a patch of early morning sun on the porch, looked at him disinterestedly. Then she stretched and curled back up to catch a few more nods.

George grinned at the feline. "I'm overwhelmed to see you again, too."

He peeked in the front window and could see their housekeeper.

Most sixty-three-year-old ladies who keep house are rather dumpy but cheerful types who waddle about the premises dusting, sweeping, chortling and humming quaint old ballads of bygone days.

Not so in the Track residence.

Tassles LaToure was the housekeeper—true. She was sixty-three years old—true. Dumpy? No way. An ex-striptease artist who had spent more than twenty-five years on the bump-and-grind circuit of burlesque, she exercised long and hard to keep her body as taut and shapely as it had been in the old days. She moved with an easy grace, and still had an attractive face that didn't need a darkened bar to attract a man; and her taste in music was definitely modern—although she would admit to now and then putting on some old scratchy seventy-eight rpm records of songs she used to dance to while earning the money for the rent and groceries.

When George stepped into the living room he could see her seated on the floor, wearing bright purple leotards under a rainbow-colored workout suit. Both shapely legs were stretched out to the side and she was alternately laying her body down flat along each side.

This was her warm-up routine.

"Hello, George." Down-up-down.

"Hi, Tassles." He dropped the valise to the rug.

"How was Albuquerque?" Down-up-down.

"Oh, about the same I guess," he answered trying to sound casual.

Tassles sat up and pointed to the kitchen. "I have some hang-over medicine in the fridge waiting for you."

George breathed a sigh. He really needed that concoction of tomato juice, Tabasco sauce and a dash of bitters. Only Tassles knew the right proportions. "Thank you, dear."

"You're welcome," Tassles said. Down-up-down. "There's another surprise out there, too." Down-up-down.

"What's that?" George asked.

Down-up-down. "Now if I told you it wouldn't be a surprise, would it?" Down-up-down.

"Nope, I guess not." George started to go to the kitchen, then stopped. "Oh, hell! Dan isn't back, is he?"

"You'll have to go see what it is for yourself." Down-up-down. "And don't forget to put a raw egg in the hangover medicine."

George walked around her and headed for the kitchen thinking of the relief waiting for him in Tassles's remedy. He pushed through the door and stopped cold.

"Zulu!"

The big black man was busy frying eggs, but he glanced over at George with a wide grin on his ebony face. "Hello, George. So good to see you again."

George walked over and they locked hands hard and sincerely.

"Hey! No hello for me?" Desiree Goth leaned out of the breakfast nook and smiled a greeting. She looked radiantly beautiful with her thick, black tresses cascading to the red blouse she wore. She was a younger, darker version of Tassles LaToure. "How are you, George? And where's that uncle of yours?"

"San Diego," George answered. He went to her and embraced her hard. "And, boy, is he gonna be mad when he finds you're here and he's away out there on the West Coast."

"I say, George!" said Zulu, an Oxford-educated man whose cultured background was reflected in his upper-class British accent. "Would you care for an egg?"

George turned to him, then laughed. "Right! A raw one."

"Raw!" Zulu exclaimed. "Are you mad then?"

George went to the refrigerator and pulled out the pitcher of Tassles's medicine. "Put it in here. Tassles cures hangovers with this concoction."

"Suit yourself," Zulu said. He nimbly picked up an egg in one huge hand and cracked it on the skillet. He moved over to the pitcher and opened it to let the contents plop into Tassles's mixture.

George stirred it up, then quickly downed the drink without pause. His stomach heaved, rumbled and almost sent the stuff back up, but suddenly it quieted down. George sighed. "Aaahhh!"

Zulu laughed as he served the eggs he'd cooked onto two plates. "Well, it does seem to do the trick."

"That it does," George agreed. He followed the black man into the nook and joined the two of them at breakfast. "So what brings you here? A gun-running job in or out of Mexico?"

"We're not plying our regular trade," Desiree answered. "Sir Abner contacted us and said we were to meet him here. Something to do with the Consortium."

"Jesus!" George said. "Dan's somewhere in San Diego. He might even be doing some deep-sea fishing or something—or visiting Tijuana. . . ."

Desiree's eyes narrowed. "If he's down there, he'd better be playing the good little *turista* and not making whoopee with any senoritas."

George shrugged. He didn't want to get caught in the middle of any lovers' quarrel—particularly between Dan Track and Desiree Goth. The lady was tough enough to hold her own in just about any situation.

"I think it would be wise to contact the major as quickly as possible," Zulu said. "Do you know where he's staying?"

"Nope," George answered. He hesitated as his stomach started to rebel again. But it settled into a low rumbling, then subsided. "I took him to Albuquerque to the airport. He was supposed to give us a call or write, but we haven't heard a word."

"What took him to San Diego?" Desiree asked.

"An old army buddy wrote him a letter and invited him out," George said. "What the hell did Sir Abner want?"

"He has a job for us," Zulu answered. "One that requires great precision and coordination to pull it off successfully."

George smiled. "That's Sir Abner's way of saying it's a hairy fucking situation."

Zulu laughed. "Right."

"We'll wait here for word from Dan," Desiree said. Her expression wasn't happy. "And he'd damned well better have a good explanation for dropping out of sight like this!"

Before George could make any remarks in defence of his uncle, Tassles came into the room. She was perspiring slightly and had a towel around her neck. "Anybody interested in watching that news conference when it comes on in an hour or so?"

"Which one is that?" George asked. "The president have something to announce?"

"No, it's that Apache leader," Tassles said. "Everybody's real curious about who he is and what he's got to say."

"What's all this about?" Desiree asked. "Zulu and I've come in from—" she hesitated and winked at George "—well, we've come in from overseas."

"Hell, honey," Tassles said, "the United States is damned close to opening the Indian Wars all over again. There's a standoff between the authorities and a small tribe of Apaches over in Arizona."

"Oh, balls!" George sneered. "It's all bullshit. Every limousine liberal in Hollywood's out there getting his picture taken and grabbing all the free publicity there is."

"There's been a gunfight, wiseguy," Tassles said, "and there might be more."

"No there won't," George said continuing to scoff. "The big ballyhoo's gone down now. There'll be concessions and all that stuff. Everything's over but the shouting—mark my words!"

"Well, I'm going to watch it," Tassles said testily. She looked at Desiree and Zulu. "Care to join me?"

"No thank you," Desiree said. "I don't think there's anything going on there that would really interest me."

THE MIDMORNING SUN was already warm, but neither Dan Track nor Steve Aguila noticed it.

They were situated on opposite sides of the small stronghold, each lost deep within himself. Track breathed in deep, letting his *ki*—that projected inner strength—build up and expand outwardly through his being from the *hara* in the abdomen. It is here that a man's strongest and most profound forces are centered.

This was one of the basic skills of true martial arts—and the most difficult to develop to its fullness.

Track was alert without wakefulness. No enemy could have sneaked up on him, yet he slept in a meditative twilight. This process did more than build up his strength. It gave him a reserve to call on in cases of peril, and it attuned his mental processes to blend in perfectly to control that coiled force.

He continued to meditate, while Steve Aguila practiced the mental preparation that Apache warriors had done for more than a thousand years. The Spirit Woman and Thunder Eagle, from whom all Apaches were descended, called him to them and prepared him for battle.

THE BATTERIES OF CAMERAS, their lenses like the cannon muzzles of a sloppily deployed artillery battery, were aimed straight on the stand of over two dozen microphones that stood five yards beyond the police barricades.

The array of mikes looked stark and dead like so many plucked limbs of dying bushes, but a closer inspection would have found each very much alive and waiting.

The air of expectancy and suspense was so strong in the area that the normally boisterous journalists spoke in low, hurried tones, casting impatient glances down the highway that led to the Indian reservation.

Turnbull and Perez stood on the other side of the sawhorses used to close off the road. Turnbull spat. "Well, the big chief will soon appear."

Perez checked his watch. "Not quite noon yet. Reckon he'll be late?"

Turnbull smirked. "Hell, yes. Just to keep that bunch of assholes in their right places." He pointed to the newsmen, then he swung his finger over to another group. "And them too." He indicated the spot where Jerome Courtney, Myra Hawkins, Wayne Harrison and Senator Ted O'Connor stood.

"I'll bet that politico has made more speeches in the last twenty-four hours than he has the whole year previously," Perez said. "He's playing this thing for all its worth."

"You bet," Turnbull said. "Don't forget, buddy, they have presidential conventions every four years." He shook his head in disgust. "And to think of the times I've driven this road on duty. I never figured things would come to this."

"Say! That's right," Perez said suddenly remembering. "That reservation was your beat, wasn't it?"

"I didn't have any jurisdiction there," Turnbull said. "But I acted as liaison between the Indian police and our department."

"Did you know this big chief of theirs?"

"Nope," Turnbull admitted. "And I never heard of him either. The only 'chief' I knew was the chief of police. He was a good guy, but they say he started hitting the bottle and finally wandered off some time ago."

"Was he a good cop?"

"The best," Turnbull said with conviction. "A real bad-ass too. Served with the Berets in Vietnam."

"Maybe it's a good thing he's gone, huh?" Perez pondered. "We don't need anybody like that to tangle with if this thing blows wide open."

"There's a couple o' more ex-Green Berets in that tribe," Turnbull said. "Along with dozens of ex-marines, ex-paratroopers, ex-SEALS, and ex-you name it. These Llanero Apaches are tough dudes, baby."

"Shit!" Perez said in open admiration.

A sudden murmur from the crowd caught their attention. The two cops looked back toward the reservation. They could make out a couple of vehicles coming toward them through the dancing heat haze that shimmered on the highway.

"The Numbah-One Honcho is on his merry way," Turnbull said.

Three trucks, the Willys that Roberto Lobo normally rode in and two pickups, pulled to a stop thirty yards down the road. A group of Indians could be seen getting out of the vehicles and standing on the highway. After a few moments of conversation, they formed up and walked slowly toward the waiting newspeople.

Red camera lights came on and a buzzing of conversation began to rise until one quick thinker shouted out, "Quiet! Quiet, please! There's sound cued now."

As the Indians drew nearer it could clearly be seen that they numbered a dozen. They walked defiantly, almost swaggering, as they drew closer. All were armed. Most carried various sporting rifles and carbines, but a couple brandished what appeared to be AR-15 or M-16 rifles.

The group halted fifteen yards from the microphones. The crowd could see Roberto Lobo step forward. He beckoned to Courtney and the other celebrities who hurried toward him.

Turnbull spat. "They get to kiss the big chief's ass."

"Yeah," Perez said. "What a thrill for 'em."

After a few moments, Lobo's and Courtney's group walked to the microphones. While the whites stood back respectfully, Lobo stepped forward. "It is my pleasure to introduce the spiritual and war leader of the Llanero Apache Tribe. He is here to make a declaration. He will neither answer or tolerate any questions." He emphasized the last point with a long stare at the newspeople. "I am proud to present Geronimo Ferril."

The crowd gave an involuntary gasp, when Ferril stepped from behind the other Apaches and led them forward. His physical appearance was impressive and savage, yet even at that distance he exhibited a charisma the journalists knew would make good copy.

Ferril, like his fellow Indians, was dressed in authentic garb of their tribe. Brightly colored cotton shirts, breechcloths, knee-high moccasins, and ammunition bandoliers were the order of the day. Ferril displayed no fancier dress than the others; in fact, the only difference in his appearance was that he was unarmed.

The newsmen saw the stocky, nearly bow-legged, powerfully muscled man stop at the microphones. His eyes were angry slits and his mouth a slash of white teeth. He finally spoke.

"I am Geronimo Ferril," he said. "My people are the Llanero Apaches—a proud and ancient tribe with honorable traditions and customs. For a hundred years we have been shamed by a disgraceful treaty with the United States government. This piece of paper was drawn up by unscrupulous politicians and opportunists. They took away our land and forced us to go to a desolate piece of the Arizona desert to be paupers and beggars, forced to take grudging handouts from a heartless bureaucracy. We had no official or legal status other than that of being a conquered tribe of Indians. Of course, during the presidency of Dwight D. Eisenhower, we were granted the dubious honor of citizenship of the United States."

He paused for effect, looking into the cameras that recorded his image to be telecast to the world's public. "We, the Llanero Apaches, do here and now repudiate, denounce and deny that citizenship, and particularly the treaty that turned us from a proud warrior people to penniless farmers. As of this moment, we declare ourselves a sovereign nation—independent from the United States and its laws—bound to no one but ourselves."

"You're making a Declaration of Independence?" a reporter shouted.

"Are you at war with the United States, sir?" another asked in a loud, excited voice.

Ferril ignored them. "We, the men, women and children of the Llanero Apache Nation, do publicly make an oath to our sacred Spirit Woman and Thunder Eagle, our mother and father, that we will fight to the death if any outside force seeks to restrict or deny us our right of sovereignty."

The newsmen tried to surge forward, but Turnbull, Perez and the other cops pushed them back behind the barricades.

Geronimo Ferril gave the crowd one more look. "There is nothing else I have to say!" He turned and walked past Courtney and his group. Lobo joined him and the two Apaches returned to their vehicles.

An incredible five seconds of shocked silence followed. Then the journalists leaped to life and raced for their cars to get the precious tapes and sound tracks onto overnight expresses to their stations. The newspaper and magazine people raced for Orv Lingenfelder's telephone in the diner.

18

The pilot, Hank Wurlin, a scrawny middle-aged man, applied left rudder as he gently turned the wheel of the twin-engine Beechcraft to change his course for the north.

He lowered the nose into a gentle dive, gradually increasing the angle until his speed was closing in on two hundred knots. At an altitude of two hundred feet he leveled off and gave the aircraft full throttle to fly hell-for-leather out of Mexico and across the international border into Arizona.

The Beechcraft was capable of greater speed, but the heavy cargo of marijuana bales and a couple of crates of Russian 7.62 mm ammunition made the aircraft's propellers bite hard into the thin desert air.

Hank barely noticed the sun setting off to his left as he kept the flying machine aimed due north. He knew the route well. He'd been flying it several nights in a row. Knowing that he could skim into America without having to worry about the alert eyes and ears of the United States Border Patrol gave him more of a high than he could have gotten from the goods he smuggled into his native country.

Almost thirty years ago, Hank's flying ambitions had been honorable. He'd once been in the Air Force pilot's training course. He'd even earned his private pilot's license in college before going into the service. Air Force Officer Training School hadn't been too hard for him. He'd played their games and passed the necessary exams despite taking a few demerits for breaking the rules several times and generally not doing exactly what was expected of him. In the end, however, he graduated with his class and was given the gold bars of a second lieutenant to wear on his bony shoulders.

But a bad attitude toward discipline and team work had brought about dismal failure at earning his pilot's wings. Flight school was a disaster. "Hotdogging" was not recognized as an Air Force virtue, nor was giving the instructors a ration of shit every time they found fault. Thus, instead of becoming the jet fighter pilot he dreamed of being—or even a transport pilot—Hank served his country as a meteorological officer, spending five years stationed at such exotic places as Texas, Kansas and North Dakota.

He gritted his teeth and spent his off-duty hours, and plenty of dough, going after a commercial license in various flying schools wherever he was stationed. But it had been his bad luck that there was a surplus of pilots after his discharge. With plenty to pick and choose from, the airlines and other businesses that flew airplanes preferred to hire men with military experience.

So Hank went into the smuggling business—and got rich.

He did take one three-year fall, but he comforted himself through those long months in Lompoc with nightly dreams of his secret Colombian bank accounts that could be laundered through certain Miami banks when he needed money.

After his release he was soon back in the air, flying guns, dope, illegals, absconding crooks or anyone else with the necessary cash to hire him.

But this latest scam was the greatest.

The Llanero Apache thing had opened a wide, unguarded portion of the Mexican border. Hired through an old contact named Al Pugnaci, Hank was now earning more money than he'd ever earned in his life—adding to his multimillion nest egg.

The sun had all but sunk behind the horizon when Hank spotted the smudge-pot-lined airstrip. He eased back the throttle and let the airplane sink lower before he finally eased forward on the control column and brought the Beechcraft in for a landing. The wheels bounced heavily once because of the load the aircraft carried, but Hank's skill made the landing as smooth as possible.

Hank taxied to the end of the strip where a semi awaited. He hit one brake and let the airplane turn around. Several men who had been waiting by the large vehicle sprinted toward him. Hank left one engine running, and opened the side door. He leaped out as the unloaders climbed aboard to quickly haul the cargo out.

"Hi ya, Hank," Al Pugnaci waved to him.

"How's it going, Al?" Hank inquired. He nodded to Fish Pesco. "Hi ya."

"Hi," the truck driver said. "Another load, another dollar, right?"

Hank laughed. "It damned well better be more than another dollar. This work makes me nervous."

"What the hell for?" Al asked. "The U.S. of A. government itself has pulled the Border Patrol off the international line south o' here."

"That's great," Hank conceded. "But what about all these fucking Indians? I don't like the idea of a coupla thousand people knowing what I'm doing—especially when it comes to running dope."

"The whole damn tribe don't know about it," Al said. "Just a few insiders close to Ferril."

"I suppose they don't talk, huh?" Hank said in a sarcastic tone. "None of those dudes will tell his old lady what's going on, right?"

"They're Indians, man!" Al said. "They don't tell their wives and girlfriends nothing. That's their custom. What the hell do you think? The Apaches got women's lib or something?"

"It still makes me nervous," Hank said. He noted that the efficient crew had already transferred the goods, with the exception of the ammunition, from the plane into the truck trailer. The crates of bullets had been set aside for local use.

"Well, I'd better get on my way back to El Novillo for another load," Hank said. "See you guys tomorrow night."

"By the way," Pugnaci said. "We're gonna step up these runs. We'll be making both dawn and dusk deliveries."

"What the hell?" Hank said. "That'll double the money we're making now, right?"

"You bet," Pugnaci said. "See you at dawn."

Fish Pesco pulled on a pair of gloves. "I'll be going, too. The sooner this shit's in L.A., the sooner we get paid, right?"

"Right," Al said. "Have a good trip, *amico*. See you tomorrow, too."

"Sicuro. Addio!"

Fifty yards away, Dan Track and Steve Aguila watched the scene through binoculars. The light from the smudge pots illuminated the scene enough for them to even make out facial features.

"Shit!" Steve hissed under his breath. "Now we know what it's all about."

"Dope," Track said with a grim smile. "That fucking Ferril is financing his revolution through dope. And they're smuggling it off the reservation and into the market on the same trucks that are bringing in food and medicine."

Steve shook his head in open admiration. "You got to hand it to him, though. That's one of the best scams I've ever run across."

"This pretty well wraps up this caper, too," Track said.

"Right," Steve agreed. "All we have to do is exfiltrate the reservation and let the authorities know what's going on.

They'll move in on Geronimo Ferril so fucking fast he'll think the U.S. Cavalry is back."

"Well," Track said slipping his binoculars back into their case. "I hate to use a combination old cliché and joke, but 'let's do like the old shepherd and get the flock outta here.'"

"The heat is getting to you, pal," Steve laughed. "Let's go."

The two slid back into the deeper shadows of the ravine where they'd been hiding. They moved carefully, letting the noise of the departing truck cover any inadvertent sounds they might make. The ravine, actually a long natural ditch, ran a hundred yards, gradually tapering upward to ground level. They came out of it with the idea of continuing deeper into the desert before turning west and heading for a good place to break out of the reservation.

But suddenly the night blew apart with the flashes of AK-47s.

"THAT'S IT," George Beegh said. He sat the phone back in its cradle. I can't find Dan anywhere."

Desiree Goth took a sip of her Zinfandel wine. "Are you sure you've tried *all* the hotels."

"Unless he's staying on skid row somewhere," George said. He walked over to the sofa and sat down between Desiree and Zulu. "And the San Diego operator says there's no Steve Aguila listed."

Tassles LaToure, seated on the floor, made a suggestion. "Maybe his name is Steve *Avila*, huh? That's a Spanish name, too."

George waved the envelope at her. "Here's the letter the guy sent to Dan inviting him out to the coast. He sure as hell should be able to write his own name, right?"

Zulu, holding a cup of tea in his huge hands, shrugged. "Then we shall have to wait for the major to either call us or return from his holiday."

"Any idea when that might be?" Desiree asked.

"He didn't say," Tassles said. "There was nothing pressing on his schedule, and this guy Aguila seemed like a very close old friend. I imagine he'll spend as much time as he can with him."

"Sir Abner is due here within the week," Zulu said. "He'll be rather put out if the major isn't available."

"There's nothing to do but wait," Desiree said.

"Oh, well," George said. "Dan deserves a vacation. It seems like it would be a shame to interrupt his visit. I'm sure he's having the time of his life."

DAN AND STEVE were completely baffled by the attack. They had carefully scouted the route they planned to use to withdraw from the airstrip. Long observation from a place of safety had turned up no evidence of patrolling activities or fighting positions of Apaches. Now, with tracers streaking inches over their heads, it seemed as if the bushwackers had appeared from nothingness—as if by magic.

The usual reaction to an ambush by rushing through it was now out of the question. A killer team up ahead had them cut off. A retreat was now impossible, too. That way out was covered by another group who had materialized from nothing. Track and Steve were sealed in tight.

They made a quick, instinctive dash away from the main attack, but a withering curtain of fire had forced them back to the ground.

Surrounded now, they desperately poured back fire in all directions. Even as Track changed over his first magazine he could sense the increase in the incoming fire.

"Let's try and make it back to the ravine," Track said. "More cover there."

"Yeah," Steve said. He hosed out a fireburst. "We gotta get outta this fucking meat grinder."

Track kicked off several volleys of automatic fire, then leaped to his feet and rushed toward the deeper part of the ravine.

The roar of unfriendly gunfire grew, and the bullets passed by his face in angry spats of split air. He went down to the dirt. Steve hit the ground beside him. "Goddamn it! They got reinforcements coming in."

"Fuck it!" Track hissed. "I'm not lying here and taking this shit. If the bastards are gonna kill me, they'll do it while I'm on my feet."

"Roger that," Steve agreed.

Both men leaped up, trigger fingers methodically flexing and unflexing as the M-16s spat out spurts of 5.56 mm slugs. Suddenly Track's hands went numb as an AK-47 round hit the receiver of his rifle. The weapon flew out of his grasp, spinning violently, and crashed into Steve's head. The ex-Green Beret stumbled, his eyes rolling, before sprawling unconscious to the ground.

"Bastards!" Track roared. He fumbled at his shoulder holster, but a hurtling body landed on his back. Track reached back blindly and managed to perform a passable body throw. The Indian hurtled over him and crashed heavily onto the hardpacked desert earth.

"Hey, bad-ass!"

Track pivoted at the sound of the voice. He looked at another Apache standing in a *fudo dachi* ready karate stance. He had thrown his weapon to the ground.

The unexpected and sudden cessation of gunfire left an eerie silence. Track's eardrums, battered by the firefight's noise, could make out muted voices.

"Kick his fucking ass, Lobo."

"Count coup on the whitey!"

Track now realized he had been given an honorable challenge, and would be permitted to go into a one-on-one. If he lost, it would make no difference, he figured. If he won, they'd probably shoot him. But he'd go down letting the bastards know they'd been in one hell of a fight.

Track assumed a *zenkutsu dachi* forward-leaning stance. He, like his opponent Roberto Lobo, would move into action when the moment was right.

Lobo moved slowly toward him, neither feinting nor offering an opening. He stopped—for only an instant—then his left fist flew out in a straight punch. Track blocked it with a sweeping *jodan uke* upper block with his right hand, and immediately threw the knife-edge of his left hand at his opponent's throat.

Lobo went under the attack, spun and threw a backward elbow slam. It caught Track squarely and he went flat on his ass. But by the time Lobo had completed his spin and was facing him again, Track was back on his feet and more than ready to continue. He cut loose with the straight-ahead *mawashi geri* kick that batted the Apache off to one side.

Hurting, Lobo stepped back a few paces and again assumed a *fudo dachi* stance.

"Hey! What the hell's going on?" Al Pugnaci, pudgy and panting, trotted up with several Apaches with him.

One of the fight's spectators pointed to Steve Aguila lying on the ground. "We just did in Aguila, and Lobo's about to take his buddy out with his hands."

"What a bunch of bullshit!" the pragmatic Pugnaci said.

"Shut up, wop!" Lobo said. "I'm gonna cream this motherfucker, and if you piss me off enough I'll ruin your day too."

Lobo exploded into a charge, leaping up to perform a *mawashi tobi geri* flying kick. But Track dropped down and brought a sweeping kick of his own against the Apache's trailing leg.

Lobo somersaulted in midair and came down heavily on one shoulder. As he sat up dazed, Track hit him under the chin with a *hiza geri* snap kick that caused Lobo to flip over on his back. He groaned a bit, rolled over and was quiet.

"Congratulations," Rick Pantera, Lobo's best friend, said. "You've just won the fight. The first prize is a 7.62 mm bullet all of your own."

Standing ten feet away, he shoved the muzzle of his AK-47 at Track and pulled the trigger.

19

Geronimo Ferril had made the cover of *Time* magazine. The likeness, a reproduction of a watercolor portrait, showed a handsome face, yet one that was savage and determined. The artist had captured his subject from Ferril's television image—angry, dedicated and willing to fight and die for a just cause.

Trevor Levant set the magazine down on the coffee table. "I would most certainly wager a large sum of money that Geronimo Ferril becomes *Time*'s man of the year."

"No doubt," Jerome Courtney said.

Myra Hawkins and Senator Ted O'Connor sat on the sofa opposite them. The rock/folk singer Wayne Harrison stood in the picture window of the mobile home looking out at the panorama of stars that cascaded across the wide desert night sky.

They occupied a trailer that was part of a small village of similar temporary domiciles, normally used as dressing rooms and offices for Courtney's television production company on location. He'd had them moved in and set up as a headquarters to operate out of during the Llanero Apache situation. The structures were air-conditioned and equipped with all the latest conveniences.

Myra Hawkins, her shapely tanned legs shown off to their best advantage by the white shorts she wore, idly drummed her fingers against the glass of iced tea she was nursing. "The one thing that intrigues me is imagining the day the government finally admits defeat and gives in to his demands."

Senator O'Connor shook his head. "That will never happen."

"Why the hell not?" Courtney demanded to know. "Geronimo's got everything going for him. He's leading a righteous cause that's seeking to bring an end to misdeeds that have been going on for more than a century."

"As justified as his demands are, acceding to them would set a precedent that would have overwhelming consequences," O'Connor answered. He was being the realistic and practical politician. "A group of Indians in upstate New York have tried almost the same thing."

"But we stole the land from them!" Courtney insisted. "It was theirs to begin with. We have no right to deny them their sovereignty."

"I'm in complete sympathy with you, Jerry," the senator said, "but we must be level-headed about this."

"You're a *politico*!" Harrison said turning from the window. The way he said the word left no doubt about its being an insult.

"Now let's everybody calm down," O'Connor said with a big smile. Behind his calm expression, he was fighting a tremendous urge to leap up and knock the singer flat on his ass. The senator found Harrison to be a pompous holier-than-anybody-else son of a bitch. O'Connor controlled his emotions and laughed lightly. "We're all on the same side—believe me. I'd like nothing better than to give them their nation, but we mustn't expect it to happen."

"Why not?" Myra asked. "Everybody agrees that it is their land and always has been."

"But if the government gave in on this one issue, they'd be forced to give in on similar demands from other tribes," O'Connor said. "Why just think of the magnitude of such events. The Five Civilized Tribes would petition that the state of Oklahoma be returned to them."

"Why shouldn't it be?" Wayne Harrison said. "The place was taken from them—another example of the white man's criminality."

Levant, well educated in American history, couldn't resist jumping in on that one. "Oklahoma was not a state at that time, but that's not the point. The land in question—which is *now* Oklahoma—was taken from them following the Civil War. Those tribes—the Cherokee, Creek, Choctaw, Chickasaw and Seminole—supported the Confederate States. So after the war, much of their territory was taken away as punishment for choosing the losing side."

"Then give it back!" Courtney said.

"Yes, of course," Harrison agreed. "They probably only supported the southerners out of desperate hope they'd be treated better by them than the United States Government."

"They supported the Confederate cause because they owned slaves," Levant said. "Understand, Harrison? Those Indians owned, sold and dealt in black people."

"Well—well—" Harrison stammered. Then he quickly recovered. "That's a goddamned lie! Racist propaganda!"

"I'm afraid it's true," O'Connor said, "but that's neither here nor there at this stage of the action. The Llanero tribe can reasonably expect to be paid a large sum of money. That should—"

The sudden beginning of a large volume of distant gunfire cut the senator short.

"What the hell is that?" Courtney said.

"Oh, my Lord!" wailed Myra Hawkins. "The police are shooting those poor Indian people again!"

"The bastards!" Courtney shouted. "The dirty, goddamned no-good sons of bitches!"

"What about that, O'Connor?" Harrison demanded. "Are you going to stand by and just let those Indians get massacred?"

The shooting gradually increased in intensity, then slowly leveled off, dying down to a few periodic shots. Then it ceased altogether.

Tears streaked down Myra's face. "Oh, Ted!" she implored the senator. "For the love of God, do something!"

O'Connor's voice was choked with emotion. "The FBI is out there with the police, and the Bureau of Indian Affairs has representatives standing by also. All we can do is sit tight and wait to see what has happened."

The gunbattle burst forth again.

"I see the government's plan," Harrison said. "They want to have all the Apaches massacred so that there won't be anyone left to give the land back to—or even to pay any money to."

Trevor Levant, who didn't want any outsiders other than Pugnaci and the truck drivers to visit the reservation, was alarmed for his own reasons. "We really must see to it that something is done," he said to O'Connor and Courtney. "Someone is provoking trouble."

The shooting stopped again.

Myra dabbed at her eyes with a cocktail napkin. "I wonder how many poor dead women and children are lying out there now."

The group fell silent. For Courtney, O'Connor, Myra Hawkins and Wayne Harrison, it was an expression of grief and outrage. Levant was outraged too. But his anger was directed at the former Apache police chief and his unknown companion who still were a thorn in the side of his and Ferril's grandiose scheme.

A single gunshot exploded in the distance.

After that, the night once again was silent.

20

The bullet zapped past Track's right ear with a whack that made his eyes blink and water.

Al Pugnaci charged into Rick Pantera, seizing the Apache's AK-47 and knocking him to the ground at the same time. Pantera rolled and came up spitting mad, but he checked his movements when he saw he was looking into the muzzle of his own assault rifle.

"Don't give me no shit," Pugnaci said calmly. His demeanor was self-assured and showed that the situation was familiar to him. Although he had a respect for the Apaches that ran so deep it bordered on fear, he was more than ready to blow Pantera's head off if he had to. He relaxed his scowl. "Leave us not forget we are all pals here, huh?"

Pantera hissed through his teeth like a cornered snake, but he stepped back and let his hands drop to his sides. He pointed to Track. "That's one o' the guys that's been queering our setup, asshole."

"I figured that out all by myself," Pugnaci said.

"Well? You in love with that son of a bitch or something?"

Pugnaci made no more pretences about being friendly. "No, you stupid bastard, I ain't in love with that son of a bitch or something," Pugnaci mocked him. "Do you know who he is?"

"Sure," Pantera said. "He's Aguila's buddy. That's the chief o' the reservation police. He's laying over there with the bloody noggin."

"Aguila's the chief o' police, huh?" Pugnaci asked.

"Yeah."

"So who's this guy?" He waved the AK-47 at Track.

"I tole you," Pantera insisted. "He's Aguila's buddy."

"So what's his name?" Pugnaci inquired.

"Ask him."

"Here's some more stuff I'd like for you to tell me about him," Pugnaci said. "Where's he from? Is he a cop? A FBI guy, or what?"

Pantera scowled. "So who gives a shit?"

"*I* give a shit!" Pugnaci shouted. "Maybe he's a narc, eh? Remember what happened down in Mexico when they offed a narc? The whole fucking border was damned near closed down and the government put so much pressure on Mexico that they got pretty fucking close to hauling half their fucking cops off to jail."

Pantera shrugged. "I have trouble following your line o' logic, Pugnaci."

"Listen, Shit-for-brains, if we off this guy what do you think the U.S. of A. government is gonna do if he's a Fed? That'll be the excuse they'll need to send the fucking eighty-second Airborne Division in here. And you're crazier'n hell if you don't think that's exactly what they want to do. Our sweet little deal will be over and done with," Pugnaci said. "We're moving a hell of a lot o' stuff out on the streets now."

Pantera didn't want to admit Pugnaci was right. "You're just supposing, that's all."

"Yeah?" Pugnaci said. "Let me bring up a point you can really understand. There's some big families getting real rich off this. If the setup is queered, a coupla godfathers are gonna get pissed off. They'll send some hardcases to come looking for the dickheads that fucked it up."

Pantera nodded his head. "I see your point."

"I don't want to end up trying to walk across the San Pedro River in cement overshoes, do you?"

"All right! I said I agreed with you," Pantera shouted. "Now what the fuck are we gonna do?"

"We're gonna find out who this mother is," Pugnaci said.

Steve Aguila groaned and rolled over on his back. He sat up slowly and put a hand to the bloody wound on the side of his head. His mind cleared and he looked around him. He saw the Apaches, all armed, and Track standing there with his hands up. Steve groaned again. "Fuck it."

"That's the final score all right," Pugnaci said. "Get on your feet and get over there with your buddy."

Steve, still a bit dizzy, laboriously struggled until he stood up. His head reeled wildly for several seconds, then he was able to walk slowly over to Track. He noticed Roberto Lobo stretched out on the ground. "What happened to him?"

"Your pal kicked his ass," Pugnaci said. "So now I reckon you two are gonna get yours kicked."

Pantera went over to Lobo and knelt beside him. After a cursory check he stood up. "He'll be okay," he announced. He walked over to Steve. "How you doing, Chief?"

"Get fucked, Ricardo," Steve said thickly. He was still hazy from the collision between his head and Track's flying M-16.

"Surprised we finally got you, huh?" Rick Pantera said. "I'll bet you didn't know where our guys came from." He glanced at Track. "Have you figured it out yet?"

"Spider holes," Track said. "I saw 'em over there."

"Damned straight," Pantera said laughing. "That was Lobo's idea. He said it was just like the Viet Cong in Nam. Them guys dug them holes days ago and got into 'em with food and water. We knew you two bastards would come poking around the landing strip at one time or another."

The spider holes, dug deep enough so a man could sit in them, then covered with trap doors of boards that could be raised and lowered, had been camouflaged with sand and brush. When Track and Steve entered the ambush area, the men hidden there had sprung into action. They threw back the covers and came up fighting.

"Hell, them boys waited, ate, slept, pissed and shit right there," Pantera said in admiration. He turned to his fellow Apaches. "You guys deserve medals for all that."

One of the men, smelly enough from the ordeal to make even Pugnaci wince, smiled. "You damn right we do. And it was worth it to get our hands on them two bastards."

Pugnaci looked at the prisoners. "Once we get this shit all sorted out, you two are gonna be two of the sorriest assholes this side o' Jersey City." He laughed at Track. "I seen in the movies how them ol' calvary soldiers used to shoot theirselves rather'n get captured by Apache Indians. And here you are—right in the worse situation in your whole fucking life!"

GEORGE BEEGH, his eyes snapping wide open, suddenly sat straight up in his bed. Minutes before he'd been peacefully dreaming, but now he was as much awake as though he'd been jabbed with a hat pin.

"Wow!" he said hoarsely to himself. "What the hell was that?"

He looked around the room, but could easily tell that all was well and normal. He felt restless enough to get out of bed and pad across the room in his bare feet to check the exterior of the house. Again, everything was fine.

"What's the matter with me?" he asked himself. He decided to go down to the kitchen and try some more of Tassles's hangover remedy, thinking that the minor debauchery he'd treated himself to in Albuquerque was the cause of his sleeplessness.

George slipped into a bathrobe and went downstairs, walking slowly through the dark house. He went into the kitchen, flipped on the light, and headed straight for the refrigerator. He fixed himself a large glass of the concoction—minus the raw egg.

The day had been a busy one for him. With both Desiree Goth and Zulu looking on, he'd done a thorough bench test of the Colt AR-15 carbine. He liked the blow-back design that had been put into the weapon in deference to the 9 mm cartridge. He duly noted—and carefully wrote down—other physical aspects of the carbine, from the heat-resistant hand guard to the nylon M16A2 pistol grip.

The firing had been the most fun, and George kept meticulous records of impressions and results. Then he invited both Desiree and Zulu to take a few shots and give their opinions. The testing continued on into the early evening, and George had gone directly to his room to do the first draft on the article before even bothering to eat.

He took a sip of the drink. *That's my trouble,* his mind told him, *I'm hyper over this gun article.*

"I say, George," came Zulu's deep baritone voice from the kitchen door. "What has you up and about at this hour?"

"I don't know," George answered. He tilted his head toward the refrigerator. "Help yourself."

"Most kind of you," Zulu said entering the room.

"And why are you up?" George asked.

"It is my habit to never sleep an entire night through," Zulu answered. "It is a custom that has been most advantageous in certain situations." He laughed deeply. "Besides, I had a bit of a rumble in my empty tummy."

"There's some leftover—" George stopped talking in midsentence.

Zulu sensed something wrong. "George?"

"Oh, shit!" George said. "I got a feeling that's sweeping over me so damned hard I can't deny it."

"Deny what?"

"Dan—my uncle—is in danger."

Zulu took George's sensations seriously. "Are you sure?"

"We're blood," George said. "And something is crying out to me that Dan's up to his ears in shit."

"A bit inelegant, but well stated," Zulu said. "But what's to be done?"

George felt terribly helpless. "Damn it all to hell—There's nothing I can do! Not a single solitary thing!"

21

Pugnaci looked particularly menacing in the dancing light of the airstrip's smudge pots. His fist slammed straight into Track's face so hard it knocked the prisoner out of the grasp of the two husky Apaches who held him.

Track, silent behind clenched teeth, hit the ground painfully, landing on his hands which were tightly bound behind him with wire. He rolled over in time to take the kick aimed for his ribs on the meaty part of his upper arm. The tricep muscle knotted into a painful charley horse, then relaxed slightly and began to throb.

Track was dressed only in his trousers. His jacket and boots had been taken away after he'd been searched. Even his Rolex Sea Dweller watch had been pulled off his arm. With his pockets now cut open, he looked like a tramp who'd been caught robbing a watermelon patch by a small-town sheriff.

Pugnaci was in charge of questioning him. Despite the crude interrogation methods he employed, the hood was no amateur in the job. He knew that the practical application of proper psychological pressure along with physical punishment was the most effective combination for getting someone to spill his guts.

For the previous hour Pugnaci had been trying to kick Track's ass while the prisoner was not only tightly bound, but also held upright between two husky guards. So far

Pugnaci had threatened Track with everything from castration to cutting off his ears.

Nor was Track a stranger to interrogation methods. He knew that mouthing off and hurling insults, no matter how furious he was, would gain him nothing but further punishment. He had to keep himself as healthy as possible for any potential escape.

The two Indians grabbed the captive again and stood him upright. "Stubborn asshole," one said. But there was an undeniable tone of respect in his voice.

This time Pugnaci hit Track's face head-on with his open hand. The meaty paw, spread out, felt like frozen ham. Track's head snapped back, and he could feel his protesting vertebra crack in complaint at the rough treatment. Track could have kept to his feet, but he wanted the bastards to have to work their butts off if they were going to beat the living hell out of him. He allowed his knees to buckle and he went down again.

"Throw some water on the son of a bitch," Pugnaci said. "And gimme a drink."

The splash of luke-warm water felt good as it hit Track's upper body. He practiced a few karate breathing exercises to loosen up and maintain control over both mind and body. Pugnaci, while quite good at questioning, hadn't been around prisoners too much—most never lasted long in his presence. His angry tirade at Pantera had let Track know that the gangster badly wanted to find out who he was. The longer Pugnaci was kept in the dark, the longer both Track and Steve would survive.

Steve Aguila, also jacketless and bootless, was locked in the semi, which had been turned into a jail. He'd yet to be subjected to any rough treatment. Everyone knew who he was, and besides, Roberto Lobo, now pretty well recovered from his losing fight with Track, had assured Pugnaci that as an Apache, Aguila wouldn't sing. "Concentrate on the whitey," he said derisively, "you'll be hearing arias out of the son of a bitch in less than an hour."

Pugnaci wasn't so sure anymore. He glanced down at Track. "Get him on his feet!"

The pair complied, and Track felt himself dragged upright. He sagged as much as he could, before allowing himself to stand.

"You're one bad-assed dude," Pugnaci said. He was turning onto a new tack. After a couple of hours of insults and dire threats, he figured the subject was ready to be put into a better attitude with some complimentary remarks.

Track, recognizing the ploy, remained silent, letting his head hang low.

"I done this a lot, man," Pugnaci said. "And I ain't never seen no one take it like you." He looked at his Indian helpers. "What about you guys?"

The pair, taking their cue, backed up Pugnaci with admiring remarks that were quite sincere.

Track could feel a loosened front tooth with his tongue. He had a stupid urge to keep moving it back and forth, but he knew that would only guarantee its loss.

Pugnaci checked Track's watch that was now tightly secured to his own wrist. "You set a record, guy," he went on. "How about that? You oughta be proud o' yourself." He walked over and gently took Track's shoulder and helped him to a comfortable sitting position on the ground. "Look, it's over, awright? You proved you're a tough guy and we all know it now. So there ain't no sense in keeping anything from us anymore. Like I said, you set a record—a record! Wait'll I tell my buddies back east about you." He laughed. "They won't believe me, man."

Track closed his eyes, again sinking deep into meditative breathing, yet with all senses tuned to his surroundings.

"You know what my buddies are gonna say? They're gonna say, 'Pugnaci, you lying son of a bitch! There ain't no one man that much a bad-ass!' That's what they'll say."

Pugnaci, Track's conscious mind reeled in the name and stored it deep and safe. *Now I know your fucking name... the name of the asshole I'm going to kill.*

"Look, pal," Pugnaci went on. "I'm gonna let up now. I'm gonna untie your hands, put you back in that trailer with that Aguila guy and let you rest up. Then after a while I'll bring you out again—you'll feel better. Then you can tell me what I need to know, and we'll call it square, okay?" He affected a laugh. "Hey! No hard feelings, huh? This is my job. I'll bet a tough son of a bitch like you has done this plenty o' times, right?"

Track let himself be picked up and led over to a truck trailer that was parked on the edge of the airstrip. A refrigerator model used to bring in food, its cargo had rotted because of a malfunction in the cooling equipment. Fish Pesco and his cohorts had left it behind rather than haul it back to Los Angeles.

The door of the air-tight container was opened, and Pugnaci led Track inside and untied him. Steve Aguila, who had been sitting in the dark, stood up and carefully watched the proceedings. The two Apaches, each with AK-46s, motioned him to move to the back of the conveyance. Pugnaci dumped Track to the floor. "I'll see you later, pal." He walked to the door, then turned. "O'course if you stay stubborn, we'll turn to matches and gasoline—a lot of mean things you can do to a guy with that stuff. Like soaking your balls and roasting 'em." He untied Track's hands. "But what the hell? You awready proved you're a helluva man. It's time for you to get smart now. Hell, you done all that can be asked o' you."

He walked back to the door and stepped through it. "See you later." The heavy portal slammed shut, leaving the stifling interior as dark as the inside of a coal mine.

Steve felt his way over to Track. "How you doing?"

Track had a little trouble getting his breath. "Interrogation." He explained it all in one word.

"Shit! I couldn't hear a fucking thing inside this trailer. And it stinks in here too."

"I can't smell anything," Track said. "Maybe my nose is broken." He took a deep breath. "Lemme rest ten—fifteen minutes."

"Right, Dan, sure."

Track sat against the side of the trailer pushing his consciousness deep into his *hara*, calling on his *ki*—that inner strength that unites the mind and body. He spent seven minutes meditating.

"We're getting outta here," he said finally.

"Good idea," Steve said caustically. "There's a handle both inside and outside on the big doors. But I imagine there'll be some dude with an AK-47 waiting out there. But we can feel cared about in here. The inside and outside handles are required by safety laws so nobody can accidentally lock himself in one of these things and freeze to death."

Track laughed, then grimaced at the pain it caused his ribs. The insulated truck had slowly absorbed the hot sun's rays and now the temperature was at least a hundred degrees. "I'm not planning to freeze in here."

"Fun-nee!"

"Anyhow there's a small trap door in the ceiling toward the front."

"Hold it, pal," Steve said. "There's no handle there—the rules don't cover that little one."

"Right," Track agreed. "But I got a good glance at it before they slammed the rear door shut. The hinges are fastened with four screws—"

"Four *heavy-duty* screws," Steve interrupted.

"Round-head, as a matter of fact," Track said.

"Yeah. I'll be glad to take 'em out for you," Steve said. "Would you please lend me your screwdriver?"

"Sure, just a minute."

Steve's temper snapped. "Knock it off, Dan! I'm in no mood for bullshit."

"This is no bullshit, pal," Track said. He fumbled at his clothing and produced an oblong metal object. "Take hold of this, but be careful—one side is real sharp."

Steve, puzzled, hefted the thing in his hand. "What the hell is this? Where'd you have it hidden?"

"It's my belt buckle," Track said. "Looks real innocent until it comes loose. It protrudes under the leather three and a half inches. One side is serrated like a saw blade, the other side is for cutting. And the end—the part kept under the belt—is a combination tool. It can be used as a file, a take-down tool for weapons, a chisel, or—"

"A screwdriver!"

"I've had a lot of practice with it," Track said. "I'll do the honors. But I'm gonna have to stand on your shoulders."

"Be my guest," Steve said happily. "But let's work fast. It'll be light in another hour or hour and a half. Besides, they might come for one of us pretty damned quick."

The two friends edged quietly toward the front of the trailer. Once there, they felt along the wall until they reached the right-front corner.

"Ready?" Track asked.

"Ready," Steve answered. He knelt down, allowing Track to stand on his shoulders. Then he slowly stood up, his thigh muscles straining with the effort. "Can you reach it?"

"Yeah," Track said. He worked as quickly as possible in the dark, slipping the blade into the slot on the first screw's head. His arm, still sore from Pugnaci's kick, trembled with the effort. He applied pressure until his fingers ached. "Whew!"

"Trouble?" Steve asked.

"I'll get it," Track said. He tried again, grunting and straining until suddenly the screw gave. He twisted it quickly. "Let's hope the others are easier," he said.

"If we're going to use up hope, let's save some for enough time to do this," Steve said more realistically.

22

A large, dim shadow was shaking Trevor Levant roughly by the shoulder. Levant lay wrapped in a light blanket, the air-conditioning turned on high in the mobile home. When he finally became aware there was somebody besides himself in the bedroom, he awoke instantly. He opened his eyes to see the heavy-lidded face of Al Pugnaci looking down at him.

"What the hell do you want?" Levant demanded. He'd always been afraid of the Italian-American on some deep level. He had denied it to himself, but the unexpected sight of the big man set his nerves on edge.

"I got news," Pugnaci said.

"You damn well better have *important* news," Levant said fighting down his nervousness. He struggled to sit up. "How'd you get in here anyhow?"

"I broke in," Pugnaci said in simple explanation. "We got the two guys that's been raising hell on the reservation."

Levant's irritation at being awakened before dawn was swept away in an instant. In his exhilaration he again saw Pugnaci as a subordinate. "Tell me about it!" He listened intently as a sleepy-eyed Pugnaci spoke in low urgent tones, telling of the gunfight and the ultimate capture of the two interlopers. "Fantastic," Levant said. "Who are they?"

"The one's the chief o' police there like ever'body figured," Pugnaci said, "but I'm gonna find out about his buddy before I do anything."

"What in the world for?" Levant demanded.

Pugnaci's explanation that the man might be a federal narcotics agent was the same counsel he'd given Ricardo Pantera. "We don't want to end up with this guy being a Fed, right? That'd bring a lot o' shit down on us."

"Good thinking, Pugnaci," Levant said. For a brief moment he regreted having treated the hood so much like an idiot in the past. "There's no rush. Everything is under control. I'll leave the situation with the prisoners up to you."

"Right."

"Fix yourself some coffee on the way out," Levant said. "You look tired."

"Yeah," Pugnaci said. "I awready done some questioning." He nodded a curt goodbye, then abruptly left the bedroom to go to the kitchen.

Levant sat in thought for a few moments. With the irritants on the reservation now removed, the delivery of dope and arms could be stepped up. It was conceivable that within one more month, Trevor Levant would be the richest man in the world.

TRACK SLOWLY PUSHED the trap door open. The fresh night air tasted delicious as it invaded the fetid interior of the trailer. After listening for several moments, he hefted himself through the opening. A quick look around in the moonlight showed that except for a couple of guards at a small campfire, the entire encampment around the airstrip was asleep.

Track had one more job for his belt. He pulled it free from his trousers and leaned inside the trailer, dropping it toward Steve's waiting hands.

Steve had to leap high, but he managed to get a grip on the leather. His sudden weight made Track's damaged tricep cramp up, but Track managed to hang on and pull as

Steve propelled himself up by placing his bare feet against the trailer wall.

Within moments both were on top of the trailer.

"Well!" Steve said grinning. "Now what?"

"Let's assess the situation," Track suggested. "We're facing a desert without shirts, boots or water. There's a couple of dozen assholes that are going to try to police us up, and a distinct possibility exists that if anyone outside the reservation sees us coming out of here, they'll shoot us too."

"I mean," Steve said, "is there anything serious we have to worry about?"

OFFICER TURNBULL DROVE the Arizona State Police car up to the barricades. His partner, Carlos Perez, yawned. "Another day at the exotic police lines blocking the Llanero Apache Reservation."

"This routine's starting to get boring," Turnbull said. "I almost wish something would break."

"It'll be the S.O.S.—Same Old Shit," Perez said. "We'll stand out here in the hot sun all day and watch the TV people take shots of trucks and celebrities going in and out of the barricades."

"I don't mind that so much," Turnbull said opening the door on his side of the car, "but that fucking Wayne Harrison keeps singing."

Perez grinned sheepishly. "I hate to tell you this, but I got all his albums."

"You son of a bitch!"

"C'mon," Perez said also leaving the car. "Let's get up there and relieve the guys on duty."

The two strolled up to the policemen waiting for them. One, a veteran, nodded to them. "I got some hot coffee left in my thermos. Want some?"

"Thanks," Turnbull said. "It'll make mine last longer." He unscrewed the plastic cup from his own and held it out as the other cop poured coffee into it. "How goes it?"

"More shooting last night," the cop said.

"Yeah!" his partner, a rookie, acknowledged. "I wonder what those Indians are doing out there."

"Probably knocking off dissidents," Turnbull said. "I don't think Geronimo Ferril runs a democratic society."

"I reckon not," the old cop said. He stretched and yawned. "Well, see you guys later. Have a nice day."

Turnbull glanced at the bright redness of the sun starting to glow on the eastern horizon. "Damn! It's gonna be a real sizzler, you know it?"

Perez sighed. "Yeah."

TRACK AND STEVE, crawling on their bellies, snaked toward the edge of the trailer where an iron ladder was screwed onto the side. A distant noise caused them to stop.

"What the hell?" Steve said angrily.

Track noticed the dancing brightness of headlights on the horizon. "One of those semis is coming."

"That's not all," Steve said. "Look."

Track turned his head and saw a couple of Apaches lighting the smudge pots. "Looks like the plane's coming in, huh? That ought to attract some attention away from us."

"That'll be nice," Steve said. "At this point I'd like to pose a question."

"Sure," Track said agreeably. "Shoot."

"What the fuck are we going to do?"

"Steal one of those pickups and haul ass," Track said. He pointed to a half-dozen trucks parked off to the side. "As I see it, we haven't got much choice. We aren't dressed for a stroll through the desert."

"I agree," Steve said.

"I'm so glad," Track said winking. "I'd hate it so, if we got into an argument this early in the marriage. Now let's go." He started to slide over the side, then stopped and looked back at his friend. "I still don't want any prisoners."

"Yes, sir."

By the time they reached the sandy ground, the two were forced to slide into the shadows under the trailer. The large semi drove past them, pulling to a stop by the nearest smudge pot. There was a flurry of activity as a crew rushed forward to open the doors.

At the same time the droning engines of an airplane could be heard, the roar easing off as the machine approached for a landing.

Track started to move, but froze. A guard, only the lower part of his body visible to them, slowly approached to make a tour around their former prison. Track waited until the man came up even with their position. Then he silently slid out and crept up behind him.

An explosive *hiraken* flat-fist punch between the shoulder blades closed the curtains on the man's conscious mind. The combined noises of the truck and airplane muffled the sound of his body hitting the ground. Track quickly stripped the man of his AK-47 assault rifle and the bandolier of magazines he carried over his shoulder.

"This is the time," Track said. "Feel like running?"

"Does a bear shit in the woods?"

Track grinned, then signaled with a nod of his head. Steve came out from under the trailer. They broke into a sprint. They covered ten yards—fifteen yards—

"Hey!" A voice sounded from the vicinity of the trailer.

"Oh, shit!" Track said. He stepped up his pace as the first 7.62 mm rounds zapped between him and Steve.

"Those two mothers got loose!" somebody yelled. Then he added indignantly. "And they kilt Pandejo too!"

"You drive," Track yelled at Steve. "You know the area better."

"And you got the weapon," Steve hollered back.

"And I think I'll use it," Track panted. He reached the front of the nearest pickup and wheeled around. His trigger finger worked rapidly, spattering lead.

The yelling guard danced backward as he was hit. He spun in an effort to run away from the thing that was killing him. A chance round smacked into the back of his skull, blowing his face off like a cheap Halloween mask.

Track ran around the truck and jumped in. Steve had already started the engine. He gunned the motor, popped the clutch and spun around heading for open country. Track slipped a fresh magazine into the weapon and glanced out the back window. "They sure as hell aren't wasting time." He could see two pickups starting out after them. "A couple of 'em are already on their way."

Steve wheeled sharply, his dark countenance alive with laughter. "Eeee-yah!" he yelled. "And they say blondes have more fun!"

23

Steve handled the steering wheel in an iron grip as he negotiated the gulleys, mounds and other features of the rolling desert terrain.

Track, working left-handed, sat awkwardly, looking backward out of the truck with his back shoved hard against the dashboard. His legs were doubled up in an uncomfortable position on the seat as he held the assault rifle out the window. Track squeezed off a fireburst on automatic.

"Ouch. Goddamn it!" Steve hollered.

Track, puzzled, ceased firing and looked over at him. "What's the matter?"

"Some of those hot fucking cartridge cases are getting caught between me and the car seat," the shirtless Apache complained.

Track laughed. "Lean farther forward."

"Great suggestion," Steve said. "That way they'll go down my pants and burn my ass!"

"We're both about to get our asses burned if those bastards catch us," Track said. He cut loose another volley. "I've got an idea. Head into the rising sun. That'll blind 'em."

"That will also take us exactly in the opposite direction from where we want to go," Steve countered. "There's nothing but open desert there. And we only have a little more than a quarter of a tank of gas."

"Shit!" Track said angrily. He grit his teeth and squeezed the trigger again.

This time he was rewarded with the sight of a shattering windshield on the closest pursuing truck. With the driver hit, it continued blindly into a deep wash. It went in radiator first, bouncing out to roll end over end before bursting into flames. One individual, who had been riding in the back, was thrown into a steep dive that ended in a solid hit on the ground.

"One down!" Track yelled.

"How many to go?" Steve wanted to know.

"It's hard to tell with all this dust," Track said.

The outside rearview mirror suddenly splattered apart, then a couple of rounds ricocheted off the top of the cab.

"I'd better give that drive-into-the-sun idea of yours a go," Steve said. He wheeled eastward.

"That's better. They're losing the range," Track said. He fired out several long streams of bullets, then pulled the weapon back in to reload.

Steve continued driving toward the sun for another fifteen minutes. "Things are getting worse instead of better going this way," he warned Track.

"Okay," Track said. "Ball a 'U' in this mother and let's charge the bastards!"

Steve hit the brakes on the hard desert ground, and wheeled sharply. In an instant he was speeding back in the opposite direction toward the surprised pursuers.

"Go for it!" Track yelled.

"Do we have a choice?" Steve responded, his foot pressing harder on the accelerator.

CARLOS PEREZ LOOKED over at Turnbull. "There goes some more shooting on that reservation."

Turnbull spat. "Something else they'll blame on us, right?" He looked over at a group of sleepy journalists gathering for the day's work. They all sipped Orv Lingenfelder's coffee in paper cups while waiting to see if anything special would begin on that particular morning.

"I don't know," Perez said doubtfully. "They haven't been as gung-ho for the Apaches as they were in the past. I think there's some great big doubts about the so-called massacre that was supposed to have gone down when this thing started."

"Right," Turnbull agreed. "And the governor has been emphasizing the fact that a policeman is missing, too."

Another fusillade sounded.

Turnbull looked in the direction of the shooting. "I wish to hell I knew what was happening out there."

A newsman strolled up to the two policemen. He nodded a polite good morning. "How're you doing?" he asked.

Turnbull feigned innocence by raising his open hands. "Honest to God! That ain't me shooting!"

Perez imitated him. "Me neither. Hell, I ain't killed a woman or kid in two or three hours."

"Okay, guys, okay," the man said not appreciating their humor. "The truth will all come out eventually. Either you got something to hide or you haven't, right?"

"Fuck off," Perez said.

"Sure." The newsman walked slowly back to his friends.

Another volley of shots sounded in the distance.

Turnbull frowned in frustrated anger. "I'll be glad when this thing is finally over and done with."

TRACK, FIRING FORWARD now, was able to use the weapon right-handed. This also saved Steve from getting red-hot shell cases bounced off his bare skin.

One pursuing truck attempted to swerve, but the bullets from Track's weapon punched into the radiator, sending a cloud of steam hissing out followed by a rust-colored geyser. Track added injury to insult by sweeping the cab with several well-spaced shots on semi-automatic. One man fell from the door with the side of his head blown away. The driver, blood matting his shirt, merely slumped over to the side in instant death.

Back at the landing strip the transfer of marijuana bales from Hank Wurlin's plane to the big truck had been completed. The pilot, nervous as hell with all the firing going on around the area, climbed back into the cockpit and buckled himself in. He grinned nervously and tried to act nonchalant. "See you fellows tonight." He gunned the engines to get the manifold pressure up, switching the fuel mixture control to auto-rich.

Out on the desert, Track was once again "riding shotgun" in a backward position, firing as best he could at the elusive targets afforded by the two pursuing pickups. Now down to two magazines in the bandolier, he decided to make the one in the weapon count as much as possible.

"Go to the left!" he yelled to Steve. The muzzle of the Russian weapon wavered slightly as he fought to keep it on an even level. "Weave right! Now left!"

Steve complied and Track fired a burst of six rounds. Two hit the ground, the third smacked a rock and hit the hood ornament of the chaser, the fourth went off into the air; the fifth went into a front tire while the sixth joined the fourth in a flight to nowhere.

The tire deflated immediately and the driver lost control. The truck whipped around and rolled, its door flying off. The driver was thrown clear, but the passenger, his AK-47 hurtling away, was caught half-in and half-out. He was beaten to a progressively bloodier pulp each time the vehicle landed on him in its violet rolls. By the time it stopped, he was nothing but a messy hunk of meat splattered along the entire right side of the pickup.

In his airplane, Hank Wurlin noticed the men around the landing strip looking off into the desert. He glanced in the direction of their gazes and saw two trucks, dust flying behind them, approaching rapidly. Every nerve in his body told him to get the hell out of there. He pressed forward on the throttle and released the brakes to begin his takeoff.

Steve Aguila drove wildly, but with purpose. His eyes darted back and forth between the rearview mirror and the terrain in front of him as he pushed the truck along. He knew exactly where he was going. He slowed enough to let the pursuer close in on him.

Hank Wurlin, with the flaps down a quarter, raced down the airstrip like a scared rabbit to get up enough speed to be airborne and climb the hell up into the friendly sky.

Track didn't know what Steve was up to, but it was obvious to him that his Apache friend was hell-bent on some idea or another. He lent his help to the situation with fire support from the rocking, speeding truck.

Steve glanced over at Track with an excited look. "This is it, baby! All or fucking nothing!"

He swerved the truck to the left so hard that it tipped on its right tires, barely maintaining balance.

Hank Wurlin pushed forward on the control column until he could feel the tail lift off the crude runway. He yelled aloud to the plane. "Oh, hurry! Hurry!"

The driver of the truck chasing Track and Steve was surprised by the sudden move of the vehicle he was pursuing. Before he could react he found himself going into the gentle sloping gully that ran parallel to the airstrip. He went into it, then out, hurtling off the ground and into the air like a trick driver in a daredevil auto show.

Now Hank Wurlin pulled back on the wheel, breathing a long sobbing sigh of relief at really leaving the ground. He glanced out the side window, and was shocked to see something definitely not in his flight plans. A pickup truck was flying toward him—at his exact altitude.

Truck and plane collided in a beautiful explosion of roaring gasoline that scattered debris over a half mile in all directions.

Track, now glancing out the rear of the cab, whistled low. "By God," he said in wonderment, "that was really spectacular!"

Steve was too busy driving. "I wish to hell I could have seen it," he said. He swung around and sped toward the outer border of the reservation.

24

Turnbull stared at the pickup truck streaking down the highway from the reservation. "What the hell?" He reached back and drew his .357 Magnum.

Carlos Perez imitated his action, producing his own weapon in the form of a Smith and Wesson .44. "You think they're attacking us?" He glanced off to the right and left expecting to see hordes of Apaches in pickup trucks pulling off a twentieth-century-style Indian attack.

Turnbull hesitated. "Well—hell! I don't know. I can only see two people in the vehicle, if—"

Perez took aim on the driver's side of the windshield.

Turnbull reached out and pushed the weapon down. "Hold it. I don't want those newsies over there to get us on TV blowing away a woman and kid or—Jesus!" He took another look at the vehicle, much closer now. "That'd be a pretty big woman and the kid—"

"Two guys!" Perez yelled bringing his weapon up.

"Wait a minute, will you, Charlie?" Turnbull asked. The truck drew closer. "There's something familiar about the driver."

"Okay, I'm under control, but I'm not letting up," Perez said. He kept the vehicle covered as it approached.

The pickup finally stopped, and two individuals, barefoot and without shirts, stepped out holding their hands high. "Don't shoot!" one yelled. "I'm Chief Aguila of the reservation police."

Turnbull walked forward until he recognized him. "By God, Steve! I heard you went on a long tear."

"You might've heard a lot o' things," Steve said. "I've been working against that son of a bitch Ferril." Then he added in quick explanation. "This guy's Dan Track. He's an old army buddy of mine. He lent me a hand. I'm still the legal chief of police."

"What are you two—"

"Has there been a semi through here?"

"No," Turnbull answered, "but we have one on the schedule."

Steve looked at Dan. "We beat the bastard here."

"Hey," Turnbull said. "What are you—"

"Hell, yes, we beat him," Track said. "We came cross-country, remember?"

Turnbull persisted. "What are—"

"You got to stop that truck, Tim," Steve said.

"No way," Turnbull said. "I've already had my ass in a sling for that."

"This one is full of marijuana, man," Track said. "That's what the bastards have been doing all through this fucking revolution thing. Bringing in food and medicine, but hauling out dope."

"Yeah," Steve echoed. "They've had regular deliveries to the reservation by air from Mexico."

"What—" Turnbull started to say.

Track interrupted him. "The semi that's coming out is loaded with dope."

Turnbull looked at Perez. "What do you say?"

"If these two guys are wrong, then the news people are gonna crucify us," Perez responded. "Not to mention our beloved captain."

Turnbull pointed to Steve. "This is the chief of police I told you about. He's an all right guy."

"But what about the captain?" Perez asked.

The sound of an approaching truck could be heard coming in from the reservation.

"Fuck the captain," Turnbull said. He looked at Perez. "I'm not asking you to be in on this if you don't want to be."

Carlos Perez didn't hesitate. "I'm your partner, Tim."

Turnbull laughed. "Okay, Charlie. Let's get our asses in a sling together."

"We'll back you up," Steve said.

"With what?" Turnbull asked. "You're both half naked."

"We have a little something in the truck," Track assured him.

Within five minutes the big semi, with two men in the cab, pulled up to the barricade. They waited, as usual, for the barricade to be opened.

"Outta the truck!" Turnbull commanded.

"Hey!" Fish Pesco yelled down. "What's the big idea? Open them fucking sawhorses up, copper!"

Turnbull raised his revolver and smiled pleasantly. "Please get out of the truck or I'll blow your fucking head off."

"Yes, sir," Pesco said. He opened the door and climbed down to the highway.

The passenger, another hardcase, stepped to the road. He was startled to feel something hard jammed against his back. Track, the AK-47 nudging the man's spine, spoke softly. "Piss me off and I blow you away, asshole."

Turnbull and Perez grabbed Pesco and pushed him around to the back as Track and Steve did the same to the man on the other side. They all met at the rear doors.

"Open up," Turnbull said.

"Hey, didn't you get your ass chewed out about this awready?" Pesco asked.

Track stepped forward and aimed the assault rifle at Pesco's crotch. "Want shredded beef for balls?"

"I'll open up," Pesco said. He swallowed hard, his face twitching with anticipation and anger as Track stepped back. Then he smiled. "Hey, fellers, there ain't nothing in there. Let's forget this and we won't say nothing." He looked at his buddy. "Right, Eddy?"

Eddy didn't say anything. He felt too sick.

"Open up," Turnbull repeated.

Pesco turned and started to reach up to the door handle. He suddenly spun, coming around with a snub-nose revolver pulled from his shoulder holster.

Track's weapon chattered on full-auto while Turnbull and Perez pumped three rounds each. Pesco bounced off the back of the truck and fell face first to the macadam. Blood seeped out from beneath him in a rapidly expanding pool.

Turnbull, his face pinched in fury, cursed. "Shit! We shoulda searched the bastard!"

"We didn't have time," Perez reminded him.

Track motioned to Eddy. "Open the fucking door!"

The man literally leaped to comply. The metal portal was swung wide, revealing several bales of marijuana. The hood looked at his dead partner, then began shaking with fear. "I'll tell you all about it, man, no shit! Lemme cop a plea, okay? I won't hold nothing back, honest to God!"

Television taping machines whirred and flashbulbs popped in the early morning light. Behind the newsmen, walking back toward the Mercedes he'd just driven up and parked, Al Pugnaci moved rapidly with purpose but without panic.

25

The Lear jet's engines, sucking in the hot Arizona air from the front, pushed out even hotter blasts toward the rear as it idled on the tarmac of the Sierra Vista airport.

The pilot had been called in his motel room a brief half hour before and ordered to prepare for immediate departure. The owner and operator of Sherman's Flying Service wasn't told what the reason was, but he was still enough of a marine to respond quickly and efficiently when there was even the hint of an emergency. Sitting in the cockpit, Sherman caught sight of Trevor Levant's limousine speeding through the airport gates. When the car drew up along side the aircraft, Sherman cut the port engine to allow Levant and his group to safely approach the boarding steps.

Something strange—almost disturbing—was visible in the appearance of the people. All, with the exception of Pugnaci, seemed to have dressed hastily, and from the way Jerome Courtney, Myra Hawkins, Senator O'Connor and Wayne Harrison hurried in front of Levant and Pugnaci, it appeared they were being herded along.

Sherman felt the airplane shake as the people boarded. He slipped from his seat and stepped into the passenger section. Then he noticed the pistols. "What the hell's going on?" he demanded.

Pugnaci snarled and leveled the .45 on the pilot's midsection. "Get your ass up there and take this baby into the wild blue yonder, Fly Boy."

"Shoot me, asshole, and this bird doesn't go anywhere," Sherman said coolly.

"Okay," Pugnaci said agreeably. He swung the weapon toward Harrison. "I'll shoot him if you don't get us up in the air."

Harrison wailed, "Oh, God, do what he says!"

Sherman noted that Pugnaci seemed cool and determined. He didn't want to excite the man, so he became cooperative. "Sure, Mr. Pugnaci. Whatever you want."

"Yes, indeed. Do as Mr. Pugnaci says," Levant urged him. "We are most serious."

Jerome Courtney plopped himself down in the nearest seat. He looked beseechingly at the man he had considered a close friend. "For the love of God, Trevor, please explain yourself!"

Myra Hawkins, frightened but confused, smiled weakly at him. "Is this a joke, Trevor?" She looked hopefully at Courtney. "Are we on a TV show, Jerry? Tell me we are—please!"

Courtney bowed his head into his hands. "God!"

Senator Ted O'Connor, his face unsmiling, said nothing. He stood silently until Pugnaci motioned him to sit beside Courtney. He complied wordlessly.

Sherman took another look at the group. Two words leaped into his mind, "hostages" and "skyjacking", but the idea of a man getting into a plane he had chartered, then forcing it to go somewhere made absolutely no sense. There wasn't much choice in what he had to do, however. Sherman turned and went up to the cockpit.

"Go with Sherman," Levant said to Pugnaci. "And listen to whatever he says through the earphones. I'll put on the set back here at the flight attendant's seat so I can hear too. Let him know that if there's any funny business we will not hesitate to shoot these people."

"You and me, we'll be able to talk, right?" Pugnaci asked.

"Of course. There's a microphone here."

"Good, 'cause I want to say a coupla things to you," he remarked. Then he turned and hurried forward.

Levant sat in the rear seat. He waved the pistols at his unwilling guests. "Please keep your eyes to the front. I really have no desire to communicate with any of you any more than is absolutely necessary. Thank you."

Within moments the plane rolled down the airport's one runway and climbed rapidly into the midmorning sky. Sherman's voice came over the intercom. "Any particular place you want me to fly you?"

"John Wayne Airport," Levant answered calmly. "Since it is your home base in Orange County, I believe you know the way."

Sherman made no reply, but Pugnaci cut in. "Listen, Mr. Levant. I still say we should head straight for Mexico. Hell, Hank Wurlin's been flying outta El Novillo. We got contacts there and—"

"My dear Al," Levant said, "I must admit that my respect for you is growing more and more, but I insist we stop off in California on our way out of the country. There are valuable papers, a good bit of gold and other things necessary for a successful escape into South America."

"But—"

"The risk is not so great at this point, provided we maintain control over these people," Levant continued. "Until Ferril is arrested and thoroughly interrogated, there is no way to positively link me with him. Remember my modest anonymity in helping the Native Americans? Now it pays off."

"Okay, Mr. Levant," Pugnaci said. "I hope you're right."

"Not to worry, Al," Levant said serenely. "I most assuredly am. And even if we get crowded a bit, we can still bargain our way out of the country with this crowd."

Pugnaci still didn't like the idea, but he remained silent. He stuck his pistol next to Sherman's ear. "You make damned sure you don't pull nothing funny or you'll be the first to have his brains splattered around this here airplane."

Sherman pointed to the compass. "We're right on a course of three-one-oh."

"Stick your fucking numbers," Pugnaci snarled. "Fly us to California."

WHEN THE FBI AGENTS, dressed in dark blue fatigues and carrying automatic weapons, swept into the Llanero reservation they found the place disorganized with confused people gathered in groups or wandering around looking for friends and relatives.

Steve Aguila, having stopped off at his house, was now fully dressed. He wore the light-and-dark blue colors of the Llanero Apache Reservation Police. But this change of clothing had been made only after he'd found that any pursuit of Geronimo Ferril and his two main lieutenants Roberto Lobo and Ricardo Pantera would be useless. The trio had disappeared.

But if those three had made good their escape, several of their closest henchmen had not. A few old scores had been settled leaving eight dead men scattered throughout the wickiups of the main camp. The remainder had already been made prisoner when the main population finally figured out that Ferril's kingdom had suddenly split apart for some reason.

One of the captives, an aerospace engineer who had abandoned civilization and returned to take part in the ghost dance, knew that he faced a long prison term. It didn't take him long to let it be known that he was willing to make a deal. While he couldn't hope for full immunity from prosecution, he expected leniency and a lawyer—quick.

When a lawyer was brought in from Tucson the man began to sing. He positively crooned a song of dope, murder and kidnapping, ending with the startling revelation that there was a mysterious brain behind the whole thing—a white man. But he couldn't give a positive ID on the guy. In fact, he'd only found out about his existence several days earlier when he overheard a conversation between Ferril and Lobo. He was disappointed that the revolution wasn't an all-Indian one, but he had been afraid to reveal the truth for fear of being knocked off by the hard-core inner circle of war chiefs.

It was hoped the hood named Eddy who had survived the shootout involving Fish Pesco would fill in the holes, but the punk had clammed up. Once out of the control of Steve Aguila and Dan Track, he'd found the balls he'd lost before. His fear was now of the mob—and their treatment of snitches. He clammed up and stayed that way.

Steve's work was cut out for him from that point on. He had to reorganize his police force and create some order out of a situation that was slowly sinking into pure chaos.

As one veteran FBI agent stated about the Llanero reservation: "This place reminds me of Nazi Germany just after the end of World War II."

Dan Track's job was finished. He wanted to get his hands on Geronimo Ferril, but that would have to come later. After the weeks of being a part of a busy two-man guerrilla army, he was suddenly emotionally and physically exhausted.

At Officer Turnbull's suggestion, he moved in to one of the deserted mobile homes for a shower and a long nap before heading back to New Mexico.

THE FLIGHT IN FROM ARIZONA was a short one. In less than an hour and a half, Sherman had landed at John Wayne Airport. He taxied off the runway and braked the Lear to a stop in front of his business office. He could see that no one was there. With the boss gone, the staff was obviously making it a habit to straggle in late to work.

"Let's go," Pugnaci said motioning with the .45.

Sherman followed the other hostages out of the aircraft and stepped to the ground. He raised his hands.

"Put your mitts down!" Pugnaci ordered. "We don't wanna attract no attention." He looked at Levant. "Now what?"

Levant was sure of himself. "Why, Al, didn't you know that the Sherman Flying Service has a perfectly lovely Ford van? Quite roomy enough for several people—with Mr. Sherman driving of course."

Senator O'Connor was frightened, but irritated as hell, too. He finally broke his self-imposed silence. "I demand an explanation, Trevor. This is an insane situation that has absolutely no meaning. If you want something from us, for God's sake, let us know what it is!"

"I require your presence," Levant said calmly. "And I shall have it."

"Goddamn it!" Pugnaci cursed. He was getting impatient. "Let's get to that fuckin'—"

The edge of Sherman's hand, rigid as a knife, crashed down on Pugnaci's wrist. The .45 clattered to the concrete. The ex-marine grabbed the gangster's right arm and sent him flying with a body roll. The large man, arms flailing, went over and landed on Levant. Both went down in a tangle.

"Haul ass!" Sherman yelled. He grabbed Myra Hawkins's hand and took off for his office. The other hostages, surprised, simply stood there looking stupid and confused.

"You bastard!" Pugnaci bellowed. He moved fast on his hands and knees, coming up with the automatic. The weapon barked loudly.

Myra Hawkins, clumsy in her high heels, stumbled, then fell. Sherman turned to help her, but he could see that Pugnaci had him in a sight picture. There was no choice. Forced to leave the woman or die, he took off bobbing and weaving with bullets slapping through the air around him. Sherman made his escape by running between his business office and hangar, coming out in a large airplane park where there was plenty of cover.

"Never mind him!" Levant said. He, too, had recovered quickly. "Let's get to that van."

"Goddamn it! We're fucked!" Pugnaci, holding onto Myra Hawkins, yelled at him. "You stupid bastard! I told you we shouldn't've come back here."

"My home is the perfect place to hole up," Levant said. "You're about to see what it really is—a goddamned fort." He grabbed Courtney and shoved him hard, then kicked at Wayne Harrison. "Let's go! Let's go!"

26

Track listened to the pounding on the door of the mobile home as he eased toward the window. He held the Beretta auto pistol firmly in his hand as he carefully pulled back the curtain to see who was standing outside. When he spotted Steve Aguila, Track relaxed with a grin.

He opened the door. "C'mon in." He rubbed his eyes. "What time is it, anyway?"

"Getting close to eight," Steve said stepping inside. "The sun's about to take a dive over those western mountains."

"Damn!" Track said. "I've been sleeping all day."

"Lazy bastard," Steve said good naturedly. "And there I was working my ass off bringing law and order back to the reservation."

"You're such a dedicated public servant," Track said. He gestured around. "Help yourself to anything you want. I don't know where the owner is."

"I do," Steve said, "and that's why I'm here."

"Great," Track said. "Let's go into the kitchen and rustle up some coffee so you can fill me in."

"We know who the real mastermind of this 'Apache revolution' is," Steve said.

"Hell, we always knew that," Track said. "Geronimo Ferril, right?"

"Wrong," Steve said. Then he added in a bitter tone, "By the way, that son of a bitch and two of his asshole buddies made a clean getaway."

"That's a job left undone where you're personally concerned," Track said. "But tell me about this mastermind you mentioned."

"It was a white guy named Trevor Levant," Steve said. "He and some of the celebrity types were staying here in these trailers—"

"Mobile homes," Track corrected him, "most folks prefer to call 'em mobile homes."

"I'm not most folks," Steve said, "and hurry up with that coffee."

"You bet." Track fixed up the automatic percolator, then flipped it on. "Okay. Talk."

"The guy is Trevor Levant, a friend of the Hollywood producer Jerome Courtney. When we did our little act on that landing strip and came charging out of there, he and his crony—a bad-ass named Al Pugnaci—grabbed some hostages and made it to his place in southern California—Orange County—"

Track interrupted. "I know Pugnaci. He's the son of a bitch who worked me over by that refrigerated trailer."

"Yeah? Well, he and this Levant guy took a plane that Courtney had rented, but when they landed, the pilot made a getaway and alerted the authorities."

"Did they get 'em?" Track asked.

"Nope. They're holed up in Levant's home on a cliff overlooking the Pacific Ocean. And to top it off, the place is a veritable fucking fortress, man. The cops can't get in by storming it, and it's a sheer climb up a rock wall on the other side."

"What about the hostages?" Track asked.

"I've been saving that," Steve said. "One of 'em is no less than Senator Ted O'Connor of California."

"Jesus!" Track exclaimed. "And the others?"

"Hollywood types," Steve said with a shrug, "but that includes Jerome Courtney. He's really a good friend to American Indians, Dan."

"Sounds like the proverbial 'Mexican standoff,'" Track said.

"In a way, it is," Steve said. "But they threaten to kill the hostages unless they get a police escort to the airport. From that point on they want a plane to take them to South America."

Track was angry. "If they get down to Colombia or someplace, they'll be home free. The bastards must have become millionaires or billionaires from the amount of dope they were running off the reservation. No doubt they have hundreds of contacts down there and plenty of dough to buy protection from the local authorities."

Steve shrugged. "Then that's the name of that story."

Track noted the coffee was brewed. He poured them each a cup, then sipped the drink slowly and thoughtfully. Finally he spoke. "You're sure about the location of this Levant's place?"

"They had pictures on the news," Steve said. "The backside is a frigging cliff, estimated at a hundred feet in height. I guess even the local SWAT team is hesitating about trying it up that way. Besides, they have to worry about the hostages."

"I don't," Track said.

Steve slurped his coffee before speaking. "You got something on your mind, don't you?"

"The things I do for my money are not exactly legal," Track said, "in fact, sometimes they're downright illegal."

"Yeah, I figured that," Steve said. "In other words, you don't have to worry about a public image, do you?"

"Nope," Track answered matter-of-factly.

"What about hostages' lives?" Steve asked. "If a United States senator dies, there'll be hell to pay."

"If I'm willing to risk my own life, then I'll sure as hell put his in jeopardy too. Especially if there's a chance to get 'em *all* out," Track said. "I think there's a phone in the other room."

"Yeah," Steve said. "That guy Courtney had lines run in."

"More money than good sense," Track said going back into the living room. He picked up the instrument and punched out a long-distance number. When his call was answered, he spoke quickly. "George?"

George Beegh's voice on the other end had an undeniable tone of relief. "Dan! Where the hell have you been? We've been trying to get hold of you for damned near a week now."

"Yeah?" Track asked surprised. "Who's 'we'?"

"Are you sitting down?" George asked. "Desiree and Zulu are here."

The thought of Desiree made his heart leap, but Track kept control of himself. "I have something I want you to do."

"Didn't you hear me?" George asked. "I said Desiree and Zulu are here."

"I heard you, and this includes them," Track said. "I need help and I need it now—*now*! From all of you!"

George sensed the urgency. "Sure, Dan. What do you want us to do?"

"First, get my SPAS-12," Track said.

"Jesus!" George said. "This is serious, isn't it?"

"You bet your ass," Track said. "Then gather up our mountaineering gear—the rock-climbing stuff. We'll need hammers, pitons, harnesses, carabiners and about a dozen webbing ladders."

"Sure, Dan. But what the hell are we going to do?"

"I'm going to give you the mission short and sweet, George, and I'm going to rely on you to get the hell to John

Wayne Airport in Orange, California, with everything we need. That includes the proper weaponry."

"Okay, Dan. What's the word?"

"Mountain assault to rescue hostages," Track said. "There's four of 'em and probably no more than a couple of bad guys. There'll be you, Desiree, Zulu, the meanest Apache in the world and me."

"Apache?" George asked. "Did you get yourself involved in that ruckus in Arizona?"

"Right up to my ears," Dan answered.

"But you were supposed to have gone to San Diego," George protested. "How—"

"Time's wasting," Track said. "This thing isn't wrapped up yet, and I need help *now*!"

"I gotcha, Dan."

"Then move out, young man, move out!"

27

The waves slapped gently against the sides of the rubber raft with a cadence almost as rhythmic as that of the four paddles that propelled the boat through the ocean.

Dan Track sat in the rear, acting as coxswain with his own small paddle held in the water to guide the small craft toward the coastline. The main thing he had to concentrate on, besides bringing them in at the correct point on the beach, was to keep the raft at a direct right angle with the surf to avoid capsizing.

The night was moonless, and he could barely see more than a couple of yards in front of the bow. He guided them by looking upward at the cliff, which rose a hundred feet above the water line. There was one particular item silhouetted there—the upper stories of Trevor Levant's house.

Track allowed his eyes to leave the target for a few seconds. He looked at Desiree Goth's back as she leaned into the effort of paddling. Their reunion had been brief—too brief—only a hurried kiss and embrace at the airport, then some hand holding as they sped through the organization of the mission to attack Levant's domicile.

George, rather than risk delay with a normal airline, had chartered an aircraft to fly them to John Wayne Airport. The gear he'd brought with him had been quickly stowed in a rented van even before Steve Aguila had been properly introduced to George, Zulu and Desiree.

After that, there had been the purchase of a rubber raft in Newport Beach. Then, to avoid attracting too much attention in that locale, they had traveled up to San Pedro to charter a 54-foot Bertram motorboat ostensibly for a three-day fishing trip. After loading the gear aboard, they'd headed dead west until well out of the sight of land before turning south to finally anchor at a spot three miles off the coast. The navigation gear, put to good use by Zulu, had brought them northwest of the landing beach. A brief but rather thorough study of local current conditions had dictated that part of the mission.

The waning daylight hours had been spent in a briefing, with some time used to sort equipment and firm up the final plans. Aside from Desiree, the best thing Track had gotten his hands on was his SPAS-12 shotgun, the weapon he'd missed so dearly during his and Steve's sojourn in the desert.

The other three men had discreetly stayed out of the way while they waited for the sun to slip down beneath the far waves. That had given Track and Desiree a chance to be together, alone, down below.

They'd stood in the narrow passageway between the berths, holding each other close. Desiree tilted her head back, offering her mouth for a long, deep kiss. Track pressed his own lips against hers, pulling her to him until he could feel her firm breasts pressing against him.

They broke off the kiss reluctantly, and Desiree gently held his face in her hands, then teased an ear with a gently probing finger. She pouted a little. "I was terribly disappointed not to find you when I arrived in New Mexico," she said.

Track kissed her again. "Not half as much as I was after I found out I'd missed you, too. Why didn't you let me know you were coming?"

"Sir Abner forbade it," Desiree said. She lay her head against his chest. *"C'est dommage!"* she complained in French.

"Our English friend does things his way," Track said in defense. He gently eased her toward one of the bunks.

"No!"

Track stopped. "What's the matter, sweetheart?"

"I am not in the mood with three other men just above us," Desiree said. "It steals the romance from the moment."

"They're just talking among themselves," Track said. "I'll bet they're not even giving us a thought. Besides, I've just spent a hell of a long time out in the desert."

"I am not a common tart to be used to satisfy a soldier's lust," Desiree said. "And I most certainly will not go back up there after we've obviously been making love. It might be different if there were other women aboard."

"Desiree! Don't be silly," Track implored her.

"I mean it, Dan," Desiree said. She stepped back, reaching out and taking his hand. "Now let's go back on deck."

"Goddamn it," he said under his breath.

"Don't be cranky," she said leading him toward the ladder. She winked at him, then ran her tongue across her lips. "I shall more than make it up to you later."

Now, with that promise very much on his mind, Track took another look at her dark figure. Although she was dressed in the same black fatigue uniform as the others, there was no denying her feminine figure—even in that darkness.

"Coast Guard!" George said in a whispered warning.

They all bent down, taking up silent paddling by slackening the pace and carefully dipping each paddle in the water to avoid any noisy splashing. The position was physically uncomfortable, causing undue strain on their lower backs as they continued to pull in unison, hoping like hell there would be no sudden brilliant flashes of search lights.

After fifteen agonizing minutes, Track was able to announce, "We're through 'em."

The regular pace resumed. Each worked silently, the sweat now cascading down their faces as the hard work began to tell. Then they heard the surf.

"Shit!" Steve said.

"That's what we're waiting for," George said in surprise at the man's anger.

"It'll be there in the surf where we have the biggest chance of tipping this fucker over," Steve said.

"We'll all get soaked if that happens," George said. "A minor inconvenience, but we'll be able to gather up all the gear." He laughed. "You don't mind getting wet, do you, Steve?"

"Hell, yes, I mind!" Steve said. "I'm an Apache Indian, and my tribe has never been around much water. We don't swim because we haven't had much opportunity to do so. I never learned to get along in rivers, lakes and oceans until I went into Special Forces. And then I did it because they made me."

Track laughed despite himself. "Damn, Steve. You'd better hope I do a good job as coxswain and keep us from capsizing."

Steve didn't smile.

Track felt their speed picking up and he knew they were caught in the water's run for the shore. "Give way together!" he commanded. He fought with the paddle to keep the bow of the raft going straight in.

Zulu and George, the two front men, paddled in silent cadence. Each pull was a measured beat. Suddenly, the paddles weren't hitting the water. "We're in the breakers, Dan!" George said.

The surf's roar by that time drowned out his words, but Track didn't need to be told that they were on the crest of a big one. Their speed increased and the white sand under the black cliff could be seen ahead.

The wave broke and the bow dipped—then rose again. The boat seemed to leap forward, then it hit the sand and swung sideways. The water beneath it receded, leaving them high and dry.

"Welcome back to California," Track said.

28

The small group gathered at the base of the cliff. Their personal weapons were a matter of individual preference. Track, along with his Beretta pistol, had the SPAS-12 shotgun, with the stock folded, strapped to his back. George Beegh packed the 9 mm AR-15 carbine he had tested. Steve Aguila carried the M-16 from the mission on the reservation, while both Desiree and Zulu toted small Uzi submachine guns. But, in addition to that, the pair had compact, hand-held grenade launchers complete with projectiles, in small backpacks.

Besides the armaments, each member of the team also wore a Whillans sit-harness. A small loop of rope with a carabiner to use as a safety device was attached to the front.

Track and Zulu were to be the lead climbers. Track's team would consist of Steve and Desiree, while George would follow behind the big black man. The groups split up and situated themselves fifty yards apart before beginning the ascent.

The cliff, reconnoitered with photographs provided by a contact of Steve's in the Orange County Sheriff's Department, seemed a natural to climb. In daylight, it would be easy enough to do without much gear. At night it was dangerous.

Track had decided to use an old Special Forces technique for scrambling up the face, both to save time and for safety in the darkness. He felt for the first crack in the rock. When he found it, he pulled a piton from the small haversack over his shoulder and set it in. He hit it with the hammer. Each blow of the tool made a higher and higher ring indicating the piton was biting deeply and correctly. Track hooked the webbing ladder to it, then placed his feet in the loops and climbed upward.

When he reached the top loop, he planted another piton. Then one more ladder was utilized as Steve and Desiree came behind him, passing up more gear as he needed it.

Fifty yards away, Zulu and George carried on the same task, progressing slowly upward toward the top of the cliff.

ALFREDO PUGNACI carefully glanced out the upper bedroom window. After a quick look, he stepped back. "There's enough fucking cops out there to start a small war," he said.

Trevor Levant smiled. "They'll make a lovely escort to the airport." He looked at the other man in the room. "Won't they?"

"Indeed," Geronimo Ferril agreed. Dressed in a khaki outfit, the Apache wore a holster on his belt. A magazine pouch was also there to serve the Walther 9 mm automatic. He checked his watch. "We should have some sort of commitment within a couple of hours, wouldn't you think?"

"Certainly," Levant said. "Shall we go downstairs and have some breakfast?"

Pugnaci led the way down to the living room, and out to the kitchen. Ricardo Pantera was pouring a cup of coffee. "How's it look?"

"Shouldn't be too long," Levant answered. "And we'll be basking in Colombia's sunny clime."

"Indeed," Geronimo said. "How are our guests doing?"

"I ain't heard any squawks," Pantera said. "Except for the Hawkins broad." He looked at Pugnaci. "You musta fucked her silly."

Pugnaci shrugged. "How many times does a ugly mug like me get a chance at a goodlooking woman without paying for it?"

"I don't like to pay for it neither," Pantera said. "But, on the other hand, I don't get my jollies beating it outta some broad neither."

"Suit yourself," Pugnaci said. "She's good and she's free and I'm gonna ball her as much as I like."

"Enjoy yourself," Pantera said. "I got to go relieve Lobo. It's my turn at guard."

"Tell him to wake up the houseboy," Levant said. "Everyone is hungry."

"Sure," Pantera said. He finished his coffee and walked through a side door that led down a long corridor. When he got to the end, he knocked on a door there.

"Yeah?"

"Me."

The door opened. "Hi ya," Roberto Lobo said. "What's for breakfast?"

"Nothing 'til you get that houseboy up and moving," Pantera said. "But I made some coffee."

The four prisoners looked up at him, then turned their eyes away. Myra Hawkins huddled against a wall on the floor, softly sobbing. Courtney and Harrison seemed to be in some sort of stupor, while Senator O'Connor clasped and unclasped his hands in agitation.

Pantera pointed to the hostages. "How're they doing?"

"Okay, 'cept the broad keeps bawling all the time," Lobo said. "I guess that Pugnaci ain't much of a lover."

Pantera laughed. "I'm glad he don't like guys, man."

Lobo joined in his laughter. "Amen, brother! I'll get the houseboy stirring. After I eat I'll come on back and give you a chance at some grub."

"Thanks," Pantera said.

O'Connor stood up. "Any word that you'd care to give us?"

Pantera shrugged. "Not really. But why don't you quit worrying, huh? You'll get a nice trip down to South America all for free." He looked at Myra. "I'll bet you have to stay down there though. That wop is really crazy over your sweet ass, honey."

Myra Hawkins gave no indication if she heard him. The woman merely continued her sad weeping with her face hidden in her hands.

THE SUN, though still red, was brightening nicely as the young reporter climbed into the news helicopter. His cameraman was already situated in the rear seat, his instrument warmed up and ready to go.

The pilot twisted the throttle, and the chopper slipped up into the sky, rapidly gaining altitude, then swinging out toward the ocean.

This assignment was a promotion for the journalist. He'd made a few points with his boss at the television special when he'd managed to corner Myra Hawkins for an impromptu interview. Then his bringing back shots of the seizure and search of a trailer load of marijuana during the uprising at the Llanero Apache Reservation had been sensational. Now, because of his past performance, he was being allowed to see what sort of tape he could bring back with a news-gathering mission over the place where the four famous hostages were being held.

The pilot swung south, keeping a half mile off the coastline. After ten minutes of flying, he tapped the reporter and pointed.

The reporter recognized the house as the one belonging to Trevor Levant, the mysterious dope smuggler. The cameraman wasted no time in putting his lens on the domicile. He zoomed in, then stopped and opened his eyes wide in disbelief. He grabbed the mike by his seat. "Hey! Look out there! On that cliff!"

The newsman quickly turned his gaze in the direction indicated. He grabbed his own mike, which connected him directly with his station. "Break me in for a live broadcast, for God's sake!" he shouted. "This is gonna blow people's minds outta their skulls!"

On the cliff, closing in on the top, he could plainly see two parties of climbers—three in one and two in the other.

29

Rays of sun slanted through the slits of the heavy curtains across the front windows. Pugnaci wiped some egg yolk off his face and made a cursory inspection of the living room. He thought about the beautiful actress forced to submit to him, and his passion suddenly roused.

The hood turned and walked toward the back of the house, passing through the library. He noticed the TV there, and decided to run a check on the news to see what the latest speculations were about the situation he was in. He pushed the on/off knob and waited for the picture to come up. When the electronic image swam into focus, he idly flipped the dial through the channels.

Pugnaci saw a cartoon in progress, a western movie, some mountain climbers, another cartoon, and finally a news program. He watched the early morning anchorman give some brief reports on the day's earliest happenings.

Something suddenly clicked in Pugnaci's head.

He leaped forward and switched the selector back to the mountain climbers, turning up the sound.

"Here we are, ladies and gentlemen," the voice over the picture said, "witnessing live a rescue attempt on the hostages being held by the mysterious Trevor Levant. These brave men, whoever they may be, are coming up the back way to sneak—"

Pugnaci pulled his S&W 459 auto and ran through the kitchen. "They're coming up the back, goddamn it!" he yelled.

Lobo, his fork halfway between the plate and his mouth, was transfixed with surprise for only an instant. "I'll get Pantera!"

Geronimo Ferril fetched an AK-47 assault rifle and bandolier of magazines from a corner of the room. He rotated the selector and set it on full-auto. After pulling back the cocking handle and releasing it, he was ready. "We'll convince them how serious we are. Perhaps we should throw out a dead hostage."

"You're goddamn right!" Pugnaci said. He was outraged that the attackers weren't playing the game; they were supposed to give in when there were innocent victims involved. "We'll show them bastards what it's like to break the rules."

Trevor Levant was not so concerned. "No problem, old son. Let's simply shoot the bastards off the side of the cliff."

By then both Pantera and Lobo were back in the kitchen. "Want us to take care of it, Mr. Levant?" Lobo asked. "It'll be like shooting fish in a barrel."

"Your enthusiasm makes up for the cliché," Levant said. "By all means, shoot away."

TRACK ANCHORED THE LADDER into the piton and pulled it for a test. "This should be the last one," he said to Steve under him. He set his foot in the bottom loop and stepped up into it. After waiting a beat, he continued on until he reached the crest of the cliff. One more step and his head came above the top.

Rick Pantera squeezed off a stream of full automatic. Chips of rock and dust rolled over Track as he ducked back down.

"An AK-47," Steve said almost matter-of-factly.

"Good guess," Desiree said from below him as the top of the cliff was swept again.

Track, working with one hand, pulled the SPAS-12 from his back, and stuck the muzzle over the top. Holding it with the stock still folded in, he cut loose on full-auto throwing out four rounds.

Rick Pantera, with Lobo not far behind, staggered back from the onslaught. "What the fuck was that?"

Lobo, standing behind the brick wall, fired several well-aimed but rapid shots at the point where the barrage had come from. "I don't know—maybe there's a mess of 'em down there."

Pantera took a careful look. "Pugnaci said he saw 'em on TV."

"Did he count 'em?" Lobo asked.

"He didn't say," Pantera replied, "but I don't care if that bastard has the entire fucking FBI with him. He ain't coming over the top o' that cliff unless we let him."

Down a ways from them, and hanging on to the web ladder, Track caught his breath. "Actually," he said, "this calls for a strategic withdrawal, but there's no real fast way out of here."

"Sure there is," Steve said. "We could always jump."

Track grinned. He looked past Steve at Desiree. "How're you doing?"

"Fine, thank you."

"Nice to hear," Track said. He boosted himself up and fired again. "That'll keep 'em honest."

Back at the wall, Pantera slithered over the brick barrier and belly-crawled through the weeds toward the edge of the cliff. He grinned as the two shotgun loads went over his head. The man shooting could not press the muzzle of his weapon low enough to hit him. When Pantera reached the edge, he hung back and waited.

After only a minute he had correctly figured out where the climbers were. He leaped up and rushed toward the spot, his AK-47 primed and ready.

Track was trying to jam another eight rounds into the SPAS. Instinct made him look up. Helpless, he saw Pantera with the Russian weapon.

Pantera was startled at seeing not only Track and Steve Aguila hanging on to the side of the cliff, but a beautiful woman too. He quickly brought the assault rifle up, and his head blew apart as the sound of automatic firing split the early morning air.

Pantera tipped forward, then gracefully plummeted past them to smack heavily onto the sands below.

More rapid shooting above followed. Then Zulu's reassuring voice sounded deep and loud. "I say, Major, we've just forced the other bloke back into the house. It's safe to come over now. There's a bloody good brick wall that gives us lovely cover."

Track, Steve and Desiree wasted no time or excess motion in completing the climb and scrambling up to the wall. "Jolly good to see you again," Zulu said with a wide grin.

"Likewise," Track said. "Although our surprise has been spoiled." He glanced at the helicopter flying back and forth off the coast. "That's one son of a bitch that is most definitely on my shit list."

George, who had been covering the far flank, came back and joined them. "We have a typical California place here," he said. "Wide open windows in the back overlooking a big patio."

Zulu nodded. "It would appear that complicated tactics and grand maneuvers are going to be useless in this situation."

"We'll get butchered eventually if we stay here," Track surmised. "I don't know what kind of weaponry they have in that house."

"Time to call in the mortars," Steve Aguila said. "Except we don't have any."

"We may be very light artillery," Desiree Goth said, producing her German HK69 grenade launcher from her pack, "but we are determined."

Zulu pulled his own hand-held HK69. "We've each six rounds. These are single-shot weapons, thus I should estimate that between the two of us we can lay out alternating fire of perhaps a dozen rounds in a minute."

"That means we'll have sixty seconds to clear this wall, cross the yard and charge into the house," Track said.

"The accuracy of your calculations is jolly good," Zulu said. "Shall we start?"

Track looked at Steve and George. "You guys ready?"

STANDING IN THE KITCHEN by the glass doors, Pugnaci, Ferril and Levant checked their weapons, while Levant did some quick thinking. "I still don't want to risk any of our guests at this point."

Lobo and the houseboy, also armed, waited for orders. The servant, a former cellmate of Levant's, had always admired his employer's brains. Even in the joint the guy seemed to thrive and get along. "Whatever you want is fine with me," he said with trusting obedience.

"I ain't so sure of you," Lobo said. "Things seem to be going to hell, if you ask me."

"Don't talk to me in that tone!" Levant snapped. "Who made the arrangements that allowed you three to escape the reservation? It was my contacts in Mexico that met you after you scurried across the border, wasn't it?"

Ferril tried to calm Levant down. "We all appreciate it, really, Trevor."

Levant was livid. "And who got you to Tijuana? Those same contacts, right? And who got you from Tijuana up here? Some of my best damned coyotes in the business, that's who! My people, goddamn it!"

"My dear, dear Trevor," Ferril said soothingly.

"You found rope ladders waiting for you at the base of that cliff when you came in by boat, didn't you? Who the hell do you think arranged all that as part of a great contingency?"

"Listen—" Lobo started to say.

"No!" Levant said. "*You* listen! Whatever I say, you do! Whenever—"

The explosion blew in the patio door, the shards of glass slicing both the houseboy and Lobo into hunks of meat. With blood spurting from numerous opened arteries, they turned the kitchen floor crimson as they collapsed into their own gore and died.

Another ten explosions rocked the house, the concussion causing the three survivors' noses and ears to bleed. They reeled in confusion, disoriented and nearly blind from the dust that choked them.

Shadowy figures appeared in the manmade fog. One, an automatic shotgun belching flame, blew Trevor Levant into two pieces of human junk.

Geronimo Ferril tried to stand his ground, but Steve Aguila's M-16 was too fast. Ferril spun under the volley that slammed into him, hitting the far wall and leaving a broad red smear as he slid down to the kitchen floor.

Alfredo Pugnaci was the real pro. He'd vacated the area when the first explosion took away the houseboy and Lobo. He raced through the hallway and crashed through the door where the four hostages huddled in fearful ignorance of what was going on.

"C'mere bitch!" Pugnaci said. He grabbed Myra Hawkins by the wrist and pulled her to him. Then, with the screaming woman in front of him, he went back out into the hall. He saw the man holding the shotgun. Pugnaci smiled in recognition. "Hey! You're the bad-ass that wouldn't talk, right?"

"Let the woman go, Pugnaci!" Track commanded.

"You remember my name, huh?" Pugnaci said. "I'm fucking flattered."

"Turn her loose!" Track repeated.

"Back off or she gets it," Pugnaci threatened.

"I'm no cop," Track said coldly. "And I don't sweat over hostages. You're mine, asshole. How you die is up to you."

Pugnaci was thoughtful for five full seconds. Finally he snarled, "I'm Italian, you son of a bitch. That means I'm a man! Watch how a man dies!" He shoved Myra to the side and raised his pistol.

The blast from the SPAS-12 hit him in the middle with a wallop that flung the big man back through the door into the room where Courtney, O'Connor and Harrison were. Stunned, they stared down at the dead gangster.

Track walked into the room and looked down at the bloody cadaver. He calmly bent over and removed the Rolex Sea Dweller watch from Pugnaci's wrist.

Steve Aguila came in behind him. "The end."

"Yeah," Track said strapping on the watch. "The end." He turned and walked back down the hall where Desiree tenderly held Myra Hawkins in her arms. She offered the kind of understanding sympathy only a woman can give to another. Track shoved some more shells into the SPAS-12 and went back outside where the news helicopter was still buzzing around like a giant inquisitive bee.

Back in the bedroom, Wayne Harrison was on his knees vomiting. Senator Tom O'Connor, his face twisted in shock and fear, looked at Aguila. "I don't know if that man with the shotgun is from heaven or hell. Who in God's name is he?"

"The toughest son of a bitch in the world," Steve said.

EPILOGUE

Sir Abner Chesteron was angry in his peculiarly dignified way. He paced back and forth in Track's living room, oblivious to the beautiful New Mexican view outside and to the hot, delicious tea that Tassles LaToure had made for him.

"The Consortium is extremely disenchanted," he said with typical British understatement. "It was quite lucky for you that an influential politician like Senator O'Connor was able to keep the authorities from arresting you." He glared at George, Zulu and Desiree too. "*All* of you!" Sir Abner swung his disapproving gaze back to Track. "I might add that very nearly shooting down a television station's news helicopter made the situation difficult even for a United States senator to smooth over."

Track smiled. "You know the saying, Sir Abner: All's well that ends well."

"That is a bunch of bloody bullshit!" Sir Abner shouted. Then h sputtered, "Oh, gads! I'm starting to sound like a Yank."

"Almost anyhow," Track said.

"At any rate, we're paying you plenty of money. Although you're not exactly on retainers, we expect you to be ready whenever the Consortium needs you."

"Sometimes that's impossible," George argued.

"Then, my dear fellow, if you can't be ready, at least try not to jeopardize your personal liberty with the authorities. After all, we have a right to expect you to do your best to stay undercover as much as possible," Sir Abner said. "You were all involved in something that just happened to have caught the eye of the entire bloody world!"

"Sorry," Track said. He sat with Desiree on the large sofa, his arm around her. She had kept her promise made to him below decks on the chartered fishing boat. Track looked at her and smiled in contentment.

She smiled back, then looked at Sir Abner. "We're really very sorry. Won't you forgive us?" She gave George a little wave. "Apologize to Sir Abner."

"I'm—"

"Pack it in!" Sir Abner said. "Well, my friends, there's no sense in hashing this over and over. As a matter of fact, the Consortium has another fine job for all of you. But this time I shall go along to see that nothing untoward occurs."

"Where are we going?" Track asked. "And what are we going to do?"

Zulu, who had been standing near the kitchen door consuming a large sandwich, became interested. "Yes! Do tell us, Sir Abner."

"We shall be visiting Florida, the Bahamas and other points in and around the Caribbean," Sir Abner said. "Certain members of the Consortium are losing millions on expensive boats that have disappeared at sea."

"Sounds like pirates," George remarked.

"Buccaneers! I say!" Zulu joined in.

Sir Abner suddenly cheered up as the prospect of adventure loomed in his mind. "Yes, indeed! By Jove! It could very well be that we're off to strike the Jolly Roger!"